HER HEART'S DESIRE

Zara and her friend, Lynne, have a catering business, which is growing in reputation. The enigmatic Oliver Pendlebury offers her a contract, but there are strings attached. Should she trust him? The demanding, pushy Amanda claims to be his fiancée — so can Zara really believe his denial? Besides, she has no time for romance. Oliver's world is so different to her own, and her biggest ambition is for the business to be a success. Which desire will win?

Books by Chrissie Loveday
in the Linford Romance Library:

REMEMBER TO FORGET
TAKING HER CHANCES
ENCOUNTER WITH A STRANGER
FIRST LOVE, LAST LOVE
PLEASE STAY AWHILE
A LOVE THAT GROWS
CONFLICT OF LOVE
FOOD FOR LOVE
OPPOSITES ATTRACT
SAY IT WITH FLOWERS
GROWING DREAMS
HIDDEN PLACES
TOO CLOSE FOR COMFORT
DOCTOR, DOCTOR
HOME IS WHERE THE HEART IS
CRANHAMS' CURIOS
ONLY A DAY AWAY
LOVE AT FIRST SIGHT
LESSONS IN LOVE
'I'LL BE THERE FOR YOU'
A DREAM COME TRUE

CHRISSIE LOVEDAY

◆

HER HEART'S DESIRE

Complete and Unabridged

LINFORD
Leicester

First published in Great Britain in 2009

First Linford Edition
published 2010

British Library CIP Data

Loveday, Chrissie.
 Her heart's desire. - -
 (Linford romance library)
 1. Caterers and catering- -Fiction.
 2. Love stories. 3. Large type books.
 I. Title II. Series
 823.9'2–dc22

 ISBN 978–1–44480–378–5

Published by
F. A. Thorpe (Publishing)
Anstey, Leicestershire

Set by Words & Graphics Ltd.
Anstey, Leicestershire
Printed and bound in Great Britain by
T. J. International Ltd., Padstow, Cornwall

This book is printed on acid-free paper

Dedicated to the
Romantic Novelists' Association
on their 50th anniversary

1

Driving down the narrow lane, Zara began to wonder if she might have taken the wrong turning. She stopped and looked at the order sheet to check the directions.

She was about to pull out when a large silver car seemed to fill her rear view mirror. The horn was blaring and the driver was doing his best to get past her modest van, despite the narrowness of the road.

There was nowhere to go. She had to sit and wait for him to hit her. To her horror he rushed past, bending her wing mirror and scraping the side of her precious van.

'Maniac! Idiot!' she yelled to the retreating silver car.

Shaking, she stopped and got out to inspect the damage. The wing mirror snapped right off and there was an ugly great scratch running right along the side.

'I could kill him!' she stormed. 'Careless, impatient rat. My beautiful new van . . . ruined!'

The gash across the pristine, new paintwork made her flush with rage. She opened the back, dreading to see what devastation might await her. Was her precious cargo still safe? The carefully designed racks and trays had done their job. The dishes of salad, the dressed salmon, quiches, the puddings and the rest, were all secure.

The chiller unit was working steadily and she closed the doors. She breathed a sigh of relief. There was nothing to be gained, standing here, in the middle of nowhere. Besides, she was due at Asprey's in a few minutes and she still had to find the place.

Shaking with shock and anger, she resumed her search for the large country house which was the UK headquarters of the international firm.

The company logo, Gannets, in the

shape of a seabird, was painted across the side of the van, together with the phone number. At first the catering venture had seemed such a gamble. With her friend, Lynne, lots of encouragement from their families, a small loan from her father and a large loan from the bank, they had taken the plunge.

They had been in business for just two months and already their name was becoming known locally. Today's booking was with a very large international company and Zara was determined to make a good impression. The scrape down the side of the van was not exactly an impressive start.

A mile or so further on, she saw the imposing old manor house with the Asprey's UK Headquarters sign at the gate. She breathed a sigh of relief and stopped outside the main entrance. She looked for a sign to guide her to the kitchen entrance, but seeing nothing obvious, she entered the large double doors into the main hall. A uniformed attendant stepped forward to greet her.

'Can I help you, Miss?' he asked.

'Good morning. I'm from Gannets. Buffet lunch for twelve?'

'I'll show you the room and you can get on with setting up.'

The security man signed her in and led her to an imposing dining room.

'Are you the lunch arriving?' asked a voice behind her.

Zara turned and came face-to-face with a dark haired man, in his early thirties. He had striking, pale blue eyes that stared challengingly from a handsome, uncompromising face. She swallowed hard. He was a most impressive sight.

'Good morning. I'm Zara, from Gannets, and yes, I have brought lunch.'

'Good. Geoff will show you where things are. Anything you need, just ask.' He turned away and strode out of the room, leaving her gazing after him. Geoff, the security man, was smiling. He had an amused twinkle in his eye.

He was also rather good looking.

'Well now, Miss. Do you need any help?'

'I think I can manage.' She was still catching her breath after her encounter with the man in the silver car. 'I have a trolley and the floors all look level, so I'm sure I'll be fine. Where shall I leave the van?' she asked Geoff.

'Round the side. That's the nearest entrance for you, there. There's plenty of parking. You can't miss it.'

She drove round to where he had indicated and pulled up next to a large silver car. On the nearside front wing, was a slight dent and a patch of bare metal. Clinging to the bare metal, a clear smudge of white paint, exactly matching the paint from the van. She felt her blood rise in anger. At least she was not the only one to have suffered damage but it was of little compensation. Feeling incensed, she went back into the hall and tackled Geoff.

'Who drives that big silver car parked out there?'

'That would be Mr Pendlebury. Why do you ask?'

'He crashed into me on my way here. He broke my wing-mirror and scraped right along the side of my van and drove off as if the devil himself was after him.'

'He did come in a bit late. Just before you arrived, actually and going at the speed of light. It isn't like him, though. I would have thought he'd have stopped if he'd had an accident. Not as if it's his first. He certainly enjoys driving fast.'

'The way he was moving, he'll soon be having his last accident. He's a maniac. He was going so fast, I suppose it's possible he hadn't realised he'd hit me. But it's conclusive. He's got my paint on his front wing.' Zara's green eyes flashed angrily.

The trouble was, it was still very early days for Gannets and she knew she needed to make a good impression. Whatever the outcome, she must try to hide the anger she felt inside.

By one-thirty, there was scarcely

anything left but empty plates. She had received many compliments about both food and service. Her jaw ached from holding the perpetual smile. She wondered which one of the group was Mr Pendlebury. They all seemed quite young and dynamic, typical of what she knew of today's management teams.

Zara began to remove the dirty plates as unobtrusively as possible. The washing up would be done back at the kitchen in their machine. There were a couple of slices of quiche left and she put them into a clean napkin, planning to give them to the helpful security man on her way out.

★　★　★

'Thanks very much,' said the tall, good-looking man whom she had met earlier. 'Nice meal. Just what was required. We have various events planned and often need good caterers. I shall be recommending you. I assume that you're a new company, looking for business? I'll set up a contract. Give my secretary a call tomorrow. I'll sort out dates, etc.'

Zara opened her mouth to speak, but he had already turned away. Obviously a man with much to do. Despite herself, she couldn't help staring at his lithe frame and devastating looks. In other circumstances, she might even admit that she found him attractive. As it was, she saw him as unapproachable, insensitive and obviously, very full of himself.

Despite him and the accident, she was delighted with the success, she couldn't wait to tell Lynne. This was exactly the sort of contract the company was looking for. As she was leaving, she realised she still hadn't found out the name of her contact. Geoff was still on duty at the reception desk.

'Who's the tall dark chap, the one who met me earlier? I have to phone his secretary tomorrow and I don't know who to ask for.'

'That's Mr Pendlebury.'

Anger ran through her. She hated people who threw their weight around but this left her in something of a dilemma. She did not relish the prospect of working with someone she disliked on sight. Maybe she could get Lynne to phone and arrange everything. She was much less likely to lose her temper.

'Don't worry about the van. At least you were unharmed. You did really well. I'm proud of you,' said Lynne, an hour later, back at their kitchen.

'Don't be silly. You had just as much to do with it as I did. It was your cooking as well. Just because you're too tubby round the middle to fit behind the steering wheel, doesn't mean you don't deserve at least half the credit.'

Lynne was pregnant and her input to the company was definitely going to be behind the scenes, at least for the next few months.

'I still think I should have said something about his lousy driving though,' Zara continued.

Lynne shrugged. 'It sounds as if you were very restrained. Not like you at all.'

'Well, I won't let him get away with it. I shall get even somehow. He really is most objectionable. I expect I can manage to be polite to his face, when I'm working. But just let me catch him away from work . . . '

'Behave yourself, Zara,' chided Lynne. 'We need this contract.'

By five o'clock, they had completed the office chores and made as many preparations as possible for the next day's bookings.

Just as Zara was leaving, the phone rang.

'Gannets, Zara speaking. How may I help you?' She reached for the message pad as she spoke, to keep a note of the call.

'Oliver Pendlebury here. Asprey's. I need to discuss a few points with you regarding the contract we spoke of. Can you make yourself available for a meeting tomorrow morning?'

Zara hesitated. They already had a couple of bookings tomorrow and she was responsible for the delivery. 'I could meet you after four, if that is any good,' she said, rapidly calculating how long things would take.

'I'm going abroad tomorrow. It must be before twelve. If you can't manage it, forget it. I'm sure there are plenty of other . . . '

'I'll organise something,' she said hurriedly, not wanting to lose the opportunity. 'What time would you like to meet?'

'Make it eleven-fifteen, here.' With that, he put the phone down.

'What a rude man. He really thinks he is someone,' Zara muttered to the empty office.

Zara dialled Lynne's number, hating to disturb her much needed rest, but she had to reorganise the next day, to free herself for this unexpected meeting.

'Honestly, you'd think he was chief of

ICI or something,' complained Zara. 'If we didn't need the contract, I'd tell him what I thought of him.'

'That sounds more like the Zara I know and love,' laughed Lynne. 'If you really feel that strongly, I'll go and beard the lion in his dreaded den.'

'Oh, it's all right. I can probably manage to keep my temper for a short while . . . enough to negotiate a good deal. He oozes charm and probably expects every female to swoon at his feet.'

'He's obviously made some impact,' Lynne said shrewdly.

'Of the very worst kind,' Zara replied, a little too quickly. 'Anyway, I'll get the girls to come in a bit earlier. Sorry to bother you. Go back to your milkshake and feet up.' The 'girls' were two mums, who came in part-time to help prepare and cook the recipes and who doubled as waitresses, when needed.

She made a very early start the next morning and once she had finished the cooking, Zara went into their small rest area. She changed into a smart navy suit and white silk blouse. She looked the picture of calm efficiency, in contrast to the hot, dishevelled picture she had been half an hour earlier. She drove again to Asprey's and parked next to Mr Pendlebury's large silver car. She couldn't help looking angrily at the dent.

'Hello again,' said Geoff. 'Can't keep away from us then?'

'I have a meeting with Mr Pendlebury, at eleven-thirty.'

'I think you must be mistaken. Mr Pendlebury isn't in today. He's had to go to France.'

'But his car's in the car park. I saw it. Couldn't miss it actually.'

'He went to the airport by taxi. I'll see if his secretary knows anything.' He busied himself with the switchboard.

Zara felt herself seething with anger. He gets her to rearrange her entire morning and then goes off without telling her or anyone else.

'Jenny will see you, but it seems that

she doesn't know his plans. Just along the corridor there, second on the left.' Geoff smiled his encouragement, sensing her anger.

Jenny, Mr Pendlebury's secretary, was calm and efficient and obviously used to dealing with the situations her impulsive boss landed her in. She was some years older than Zara but an extremely attractive woman. How could Mr Precious Pendlebury have anything other than glamorous women around him?

'I'm afraid he didn't tell me anything about this meeting. When was it arranged? It isn't in the diary.'

'He phoned yesterday evening, around six, I suppose.'

'After I'd left, then. I'm so sorry you have been troubled. He must have changed his flight and presumably, was unable to contact you. I didn't think he planned to be in the office at all today.'

'You don't have to make excuses for him. I think I understand the situation. He obviously expects everyone to be available whenever he whistles.'

'He isn't usually like that, I assure you. I'm not trying to make excuses but he is a very busy man. Under enormous pressure. He's really such a nice person.' She looked pensive and pulled herself together again. 'However, I do know he wants to take on a regular catering company. It seems to be the only viable option, short of having our own kitchens here.'

'Naturally, we want the contract, but we do have a number of clients on our books. We couldn't be exclusive to Asprey's. Clearly, there's no point in my waiting here. Perhaps you will be kind enough to telephone my office when Mr Pendlebury returns?'

'I am sorry,' Jenny said again.

As Zara left the building, she made a great effort to smile at Geoff. Back in her car she let out a stifled grunt of annoyance.

'What a waste of time,' Lynne sympathised later.

'I think it was deliberate . . . an

attempt to show me just how powerful he is, in his own little world. I won't jump next time. He can wait his turn. Right. I am going to make some bread dough. Bashing that around will help me regain my temper.' Lynne smiled after her.

A week went by with no further contract from Asprey's.

'Looks like we've lost that one,' Zara said ruefully. They were busy enough, considering the short time they'd been operating. But they were not yet secure enough to turn down any work. 'Must have been my little outburst. Sorry.'

'Don't worry. Even I would have been sorely tried by that one!' Lynne was always calm and made a perfect foil for her more volatile friend. 'By the way, your dad phoned. He wants you to call round this evening.'

'Is he all right?' asked Zara quickly. It wasn't like him to ask for a visit. She called regularly each week and he tried not to bother her at other times.

'Think he just wanted a chat. He sounded fine.'

'All the same I'd better phone back. See what he wants.' He wasn't home when she tried calling during the rest of the afternoon. Feeling a little anxious, she drove straight to his house after work.

'Hello, my darling,' he greeted her. 'How lovely to see you.'

'Are you OK?' she asked. 'I was trying to ring you.' He never complained and managed so well on his own. It had been three years since her mother had died and he had stayed on in their home, all alone and determined not to be a trouble to his only daughter. She had offered to move back in with him, to provide company and the care she felt he needed. He had flatly refused, insisting that she had her own life to lead.

'Come in. I've got a bottle of your favourite Sancerre in the fridge . . . hoped you'd find time to drop in.'

'Mmm, lovely. Are you sure there's

17

nothing wrong? It's not like you to phone the office.'

'Course there's nothing wrong. As you can see, I'm fine. No, I just thought I might put a little business your way.'

Zara sat back in the deep armchair, sipping the icy cold wine.

'Thinking of having a dinner party or something?' she joked.

'I am, as a matter of fact.'

'Oh! Well, I'll come and cook for you, you know that. You're not a customer!'

'I have an old friend, here on holiday. Do you remember Uncle Ted? He's over from Australia for a few weeks.'

'Uncle Ted?'

'He thinks he might be able to put some work your way. You interested?'

'Brilliant. Of course we are. So the dinner party is to soften him up?'

'Naturally. Once he's tasted a sample of your cooking, he will fall at your feet. Is next Saturday any good? There'll be the four of us. Or would you like to include Lynne and her husband as well?'

'No. Let's keep it small and informal. That sounds great. It's years since I saw Uncle Ted. In fact, I think I was still at primary school.'

'So it's a date then?'

'I shall look forward to it,' she smiled. 'And fortunately, there are no bookings this weekend so you can have me all to yourself.'

2

There were no weekend functions planned for Gannets so Zara spent a leisurely day at her father's home, preparing his favourite foods for the dinner party. By seven o'clock, everything was ready. Cold starters stood in the fridge, while chicken with tarragon awaited final heating and the addition of cream to the sauce. Hazelnut meringues were sealed in a tin and the fromage frais, flavoured with pureed fresh strawberries, was ready to pipe just before serving.

They sipped their wine as they awaited their guests. A car stopped and Zara went to the window to catch a first glimpse of the new arrivals. She blinked with astonishment at the large silver car outside. It couldn't be? No, she was becoming obsessed by silver cars.

Her father ushered in the guests and

she stepped forward to kiss the man she knew as Uncle Ted. Behind him, in the doorway, stood the tall figure of Oliver Pendlebury. She hesitated and forced a smile on to her face. How on earth could she be polite for a whole evening, to this man?

'Zara, my dear. My goodness what a beauty you've turned into. Where are the pigtails and braces on the teeth?'

'Gave them up years ago,' she laughed, with a sideways glance at Oliver. 'Lovely to see you again.'

'This is my son, Oliver. I doubt you'd remember each other. He was usually at boarding school while my wife and I travelled so much.'

'How do you do, Zara. I have been looking forward to meeting you.' He gave no sign that they had ever met before and she wondered if, perhaps, he had not recognised her.

'How do you do. Gosh, why didn't I know that your name was Pendlebury? I think I only ever knew you as Uncle Ted. Come and sit down. Are you getting some drinks, Dad?' Zara had switched to auto-pilot, preferring to appear slightly superficial rather than allow anything to upset her father's evening.

They sat with drinks and chatted casually. Excusing herself, she went into the kitchen to see to the dinner. She so wanted to get through the evening, without letting her father down. Smoothing her hand through her coppery hair, she looked fully in control, despite the tumult of emotions rushing through her. She knew she looked good, the green silk blouse complimenting the colour of her eyes. It was a slight boost to her confidence. She went through to seat the guests.

Watching her father's happy smile, Zara knew the evening was proving a success . . . for him at least.

Oliver turned on his ample supply of charm and had entertained them with his stories. After gaining his degree in computer studies, he had spent several years in Australia, working at all manner of jobs from sheep farming to pearl diving. He claimed he'd wanted to experience life as it really is, before coming to England to settle down to a serious career. He was excellent company, she was forced to admit.

'I'll get more coffee,' she said, late into the evening, during a brief pause in the conversation. She went into the kitchen and busied herself with the filter machine.

'I thought I'd bring the cups through,' Oliver said. He stood behind her. Despite her high heels, she only just reached above his shoulder.

'Thanks,' she replied, 'but I was going to bring fresh ones.'

'Look, I realise I must have done something to annoy you, but whatever it is, I'm sorry. You've been throwing out chips of ice at me all evening. Positively glacial. I'm not used to that sort of treatment from such a beautiful lady.'

'Keep your charm for those who need it. Look, for my father's sake, I don't want to spoil the evening. Had I known it was you who was coming, I doubt very much whether I could have agreed to go through with it. I am here for my father and Uncle Ted, of course. It's hard to believe you're his son. You couldn't be more different.'

'I see. You don't believe in beating about the bush, do you? What exactly am I supposed to have done, by the way? To make you dislike me so much?'

Zara could hardly believe what she was hearing.

'You do know who I am, don't you? Gannets? Foods for all occasions?'

'Naturally. But our fathers seemed so pleased at the thought of introducing us, I didn't have the heart to say I'd found you already. Your father especially, seemed delighted to think we may be working together. I simply pretended this was our first meeting, for their sakes.'

'I see,' she replied, slightly mollified by his explanation and sympathetic understanding of their fathers. 'But what you did to me the other day was quite unforgivable. I rearranged my entire day, even made a six o'clock start, to get to your meeting. I then find you've gone away without a word to anyone. You could have had the courtesy to let me know, if only to save me the drive out there.'

'But I did. I left a message on your machine. I was forced to change my plans at the last minute. I called from the airport at some ungodly hour. Didn't you check your messages?'

'There was no message when I got in. I would hardly have wasted my morning if I'd received any message.' She bit her lip. Had she in fact checked? She had been in rather a state that morning. Anxious to get the work done without worrying Lynne too much.

'I'm sorry, but I promise you, I did call. Perhaps the machine wasn't working? You should get a new one from Asprey's . . . they are entirely reliable. However I apologise for the misunderstanding. Come on, please, can't we at least try to be friends?'

'And you damaged my van, quite badly, with your reckless driving. I suppose you choose to ignore that too?'

He looked slightly uncomfortable.

'Geoff mentioned to me that you were upset. I'm sorry but I didn't realise I'd even touched it. Of course I remember the incident. But I thought it was just the uneven road that caused the bumping. I'd pulled over to avoid you and thought I must have driven over the other kerb or something.'

'And you didn't even notice the damage to your own car?'

'To be truthful, I assumed it was you who hit me in the car park. I didn't say anything as mine is a company car. I can easily get it fixed.'

'We don't all have company cars. It costs us money we can't afford, to repair that sort of damage. There's no great corporation behind us, to pay our bills,' Her tone was distinctly acid.

'Have it fixed and send me the bill.

I'll make sure you're not out of pocket, I really didn't know.'

'It's that simple, is it?'

'Look I've said I'm sorry and offered to pay for the damage. What more do you want?'

Zara remained unmoved. She might like to have been friends but she felt too much antagonism towards him. She couldn't understand why it was, as she was normally a friendly person. There was something about him that made her feel on edge all the time. If she relaxed, she was in danger of . . . well something she might not be able to handle.

'Look, we need to be professional if we are to work together. Our fathers may have been friends for years but that doesn't mean I have to like you. But I really do need this contract for our company.'

If Gannets failed to get the contract, then so be it. They were steadily building up their business and would continue to do so. If they got the

Asprey's contract, it would be a terrific boost. But there was no way she would be compromised by this man, family friend or not.

A professional relationship with Oliver was the most she could cope with. Oliver went back into the lounge.

'Coffee's on its way,' he announced to the two old men, who both scanned his face for an indication of how the conversation had gone. They got no clues. Zara came in, carrying the fresh coffee and cups. As she gave Oliver his cup, he somehow managed to touch her hand, holding it there for a little longer than was necessary. A shiver ran through her body and she jumped as if she had been stung, almost spilling the coffee.

'Sorry,' she mumbled, covering her confusion by going to the kitchen to fetch more cream. She missed the glance exchanged by the two fathers and the slight smile of pleasure that resulted.

'They make a handsome couple,

don't they,' Ted said quietly, as they were leaving.

'Shh,' responded Zara's father, 'don't push them. If Zara even suspects we're matchmaking, she'll be off like a shot! I know my daughter.'

'Thank you both for a lovely evening,' Ted said. 'And I hope you two will be able to work out something business-wise.'

Oliver leaned towards her, as if he were about to kiss her too. She quickly moved back, holding out a polite hand to be shaken. She saw the slightly mocking look in his eye as the corners of his mouth twitched. Taking her hand in a firm grasp, he murmured, 'Thank you for a delightful evening. You really do cook like a dream and I promise, I shall be in touch very soon.' He held on to her hand as long as he could.

Once they had driven off, she went back to clear the kitchen. She loaded the dishwasher and set it running.

'Thank you from me too, darling. For the whole evening. It was a lovely meal and so nice to entertain again, after all this time. Tell me, how did you like Oliver? Do you think you'll get some business?' asked her father anxiously.

'He says he'll ring . . . I assume he will put some work our way.' She couldn't say more, knowing he would be hurt if she told the truth about her feelings for Oliver. There were few people she had ever disliked so much on so short an acquaintance.

'You know, the four of us,' continued her father, 'your mother and Vanessa and Ted, we were all friends together from way back. We used to dream that our children would grow up together and be the greatest friends, possibly even marry one day and unite our two families. But we all moved apart and gradually lost touch apart from the occasional get-together. I don't suppose you remember much about it really. You were quite young.'

'I did remember him when I saw him. But as you say, it was some time ago now.'

'Then they went abroad and we lost touch, except for Christmas cards. It would be wonderful if it happened now, after all this time. I know how much your mother would have liked it.'

'Dad,' she began. 'These sort of plans rarely work out. Don't expect too much from me.'

'Of course not, darling. But he's a good-looking chap, you must admit. Successful too. You could do worse, you know.'

'Dad, because I'm twenty-six and haven't provided you with hoards of grandchildren, it doesn't mean I'm on the shelf, or likely to stay that way. I simply haven't met the right man yet. Now, I must get the rest of the washing-up organised.'

When Zara arrived at work on Monday morning, Lynne was sitting at her desk, looking rather smug.

'You look pleased with yourself.'

'Cast your eyes over there,' she said, pointing at Zara's desk, where there was a large basket of roses.

31

'Oh, how lovely. Where are they from?'

'Uncle Ted and Oliver, whoever they may be. You obviously made some impression.'

'Uncle Ted is such a sweetie. Almost as nice as my father.' Zara decided to ignore any contribution Oliver might have made to the flowers.

She read the card. *Thank you for a memorable evening, Best wishes Uncle Ted and Oliver.* It was nice of them, though they must have cost a packet and she didn't like an old man to spend his money, so rashly.

'I must phone and thank him later.'

'There's more,' said Lynne. 'Your Mr Pendlebury's secretary has called. He wants a meeting tomorrow. I said the diary looked clear, but that you would call back and confirm.'

'He is most decidedly not my Mr Pendlebury. I shall be busy tomorrow. Do me a favour and say I'll see them next week. We can't drop everything, whenever they snap their fingers.'

'I see,' Lynne said, looking hard at her friend. 'Do I detect a note of getting one's own back? Don't kill the contract though. We badly need companies like Asprey's.'

'Yes I know. OK. Tell them I can possibly manage a meeting later in the week. I can't face that self-opinionated creep, this early in the day.'

'Bad weekend, was it?' Lynne asked.

'Not really. No, of course it wasn't. I've just got the Monday blues.'

'How did the dinner go?'

'Fine, thanks,' she replied without enthusiasm.

'That good, eh?' Lynne waited. Her friend would talk when she was ready.

'I suppose I might as well tell you. Oliver Pendlebury is none other than Uncle Ted's beloved son. It seems that our parents have been planning the wedding since we were both in nappies, before even. Frankly, I'd rather enter an order of silent nuns than go out with him.'

'Wow! I'll phone Asprey's to make

your appointment for next week,' Lynne said, after a pause. 'Seriously love, we really do need this business. I suppose I could always cover it myself. But then, it's your contact and seeing someone in my condition is hardly going to inspire confidence in a new business.'

It was almost lunch-time when Lynne came through to the kitchen.

'I'm sorry, but I couldn't fend your Oliver off . . . ' she began.

'He is not my Oliver.'

'OK. Sorry. Anyway, he insists on seeing you tomorrow. They've got some conference later in the week and want us to cater it. We need the work. After the one reception, we've hardly got any bookings this week. Look, I'll do it if you like. I really don't mind and I admit to being curious to see this man. It's not like you to behave this way.'

'You're right. I am being silly and unprofessional.'

3

Zara was calm, as she walked along to Oliver's office. She had dressed carefully in her business suit and was carrying a neat document case with the sample menus for Gannets. She shook hands formally with Oliver, hoping he couldn't hear the way her heart was thumping. Despite herself, she recognised that this man certainly did have something about him that affected her most profoundly. Despite herself, she did find him more than just a little attractive. He had a certain charisma.

'If there is anything else you want to know, please ask,' she said at the end of her presentation.

'Fine. That's excellent. We'll arrange a formal agreement. We may need to call on you at short notice occasionally.'

'That shouldn't be too much of a problem. We always keep large stocks of ingredients and prepared dishes in our freezers.'

'That's good. We'll offer a retainer for the service, of course. There will also be occasional weekend functions. We use this place for overseas visitors. Conferences. Seminars. You know the sort of thing. We have a full housekeeping staff of course but the kitchens are simply not equipped or modernised for today's standards. Could you provide meals for residential guests at weekends?'

She thought quickly, planning the organisation. It wasn't at all what she had been expecting. They often had weekend weddings and parties booked and this used up all their part-time staff.

'I think it possibly could be managed,' she said, not wanting to lose any opportunities for Gannets. But this was not quite what she had been expecting. 'Providing we have adequate notice, of course. Weekends do tend to be popular times for our other clients and these are usually booked well in advance.'

'Of course. Excellent. I'm sure we can agree suitable terms. I'll take you out to dinner this evening, to thank you and seal the contract. I'll pick you up at seven. Wear something special.'

Zara felt her composure slipping again. How dare he assume she would want to go out with him?

'I'm sorry. I thought we had agreed that we should stick to a business only arrangement.' She was fighting to keep her voice level and her green eyes flashed with suppressed anger.

'Naturally, I usually seal my contracts over a meal. Goes with the territory. Did you think I was suggesting something more?' His eyes looked innocent enough but she sensed an underlying amusement. Leave your address with my secretary so that my driver knows where to come. Goodbye till seven.'

Feeling confused, Zara rose to her feet and extended a formal hand to shake. Oliver ignored it, pretending, she was sure, to be engrossed in a sheet of paper. How dare he keep unnerving her this way? Fine, if that was how he wanted to play it, she would play him at his own game. She'd show him how to behave decently. She would wear her most glamorous outfit for dinner that evening and 'knock him cold' as Lynne would put it. He did actually make it sound as if it was a formal business dinner, she had to admit. All the same, she found him most disconcerting.

Despite the lack of time, Zara took great pains with her appearance for the evening. She brushed her hair till it shone and gleamed like burnished copper. She chose her favourite black silk crêpe dress which fitted like a glove and showed off her slender figure to the best advantage.

At precisely seven o'clock, the silver car drew up at her flat. Evidently the driver Oliver had mentioned, had been abandoned in favour of driving his own car. She saw that another couple were in the car. She climbed into the back where a man introduced as Richard was next to her and sitting close to Oliver in the front, was Amanda.

The immaculate blonde female drawled, 'Hi.' The last thing Zara had expected, was to be part of a foursome. The conversation was formal and stilted during the drive, which mercifully did not last too long.

The restaurant was obviously very expensive and a favoured place for business entertaining. She kept wondering why the evening had been contrived but she was determined to let them think she was enjoying it. It seemed particularly important now she had met the woman who was obviously Oliver's girlfriend. She was relieved that she needn't pretend that she and Oliver were more than business acquaintances.

Watching Oliver and Amanda flirting, she felt she should be relieved. But she was not.

Richard was attentive and amusing, allowing Zara to relax and behave much more like her normal self. She caught Oliver's icy blue gaze a couple of times but ignored it. She felt ridiculously pleased to see a twitch of annoyance hovering round his mouth. As for Amanda she leaned more and more towards him whenever the opportunity presented itself, murmuring things that no one else could hear. They were clearly much more than good friends. Zara tried to avoid watching their rather obvious behaviour and concentrate her attention on Richard.

'I was asking whether you would like to go sailing one weekend? I have a boat at the Reservoir Club. Do you like sailing?'

Zara hesitated before replying, Richard was nice enough, but not really her type, whatever her type might be.

'She will probably be very busy for the next few weekends,' Oliver interrupted. 'We've been negotiating a contract. It involves several weekends in the next few months.'

Zara didn't know whether to throw something at him or be grateful for an escape route. She really didn't like sailing, however nice Richard might seem. But she did not need Oliver to presume what she would or would not do. Her social life was none of his business.

'Thanks, Richard. I should love to go sailing sometime. I haven't been for years,' she replied, glaring at Oliver. 'But, it will have to be arranged for some time in the future. As Oliver says, I am going to be extremely busy for the next few weekends.' She noticed a smile begin to decorate the corners of his mouth. Those icy blue eyes stared back with a hint of mockery that seemed to say, *just you wait*.

Amanda was angry when Oliver delivered her home first. Obviously she'd had her own agenda for the rest of the evening.

'Won't you come back for a drink when you've deposited the rest of your little party in their homes?' she tried to wheedle.

'Sorry. I have an early start tomorrow. Goodnight.'

'You're surely going to see me to my door?' she demanded.

'I'd have thought you could manage four yards alone. But, if you insist.' He leapt out of the car and went to open her door. She stepped out, allowing her long legs to stretch provocatively in front of his eyes. She held on to his hand and pushed herself into his arms at the top of the steps. She kissed him, winding her arms round his neck. He pushed open the door and disengaged her arms.

'Goodnight, Amanda,' he said firmly as he turned away. Zara smiled at his obvious embarrassment. He got back into the driving seat and drove away rather too fast, leaving a flurry of gravel. 'Sorry about all that,' he mumbled.

They delivered Richard to his home and he gave her a peck on the cheek, promising he would call her very soon. Zara wondered why Oliver had insisted on dropping her off last.

'I needed to have a few words in private,' he said.

'I meant what I said about business arrangements.' She spoke a little too quickly.

'Don't worry. I haven't forgotten. Why else would I have brought friends with me tonight? Relax, your precious morals are quite safe.' His voice sounded cold.

'What exactly was the point of tonight's little charade?'

'Does there have to be a motive?'

She thought for a moment, then said, 'I'm not sure. I simply don't understand why you set up the evening with your girlfriend and some other man to partner me.'

'Amanda needed to meet you and Richard's an old friend of mine to even up the numbers. Besides, I'd like us to be friends. After all, our families have been friends for years. I wanted to thank you for your hospitality the other night, as well as sealing our deal. Don't worry, there's nothing personal. I shall put it all down as business expenses.'

'I see. I thought this was rather an

expensive evening. I should have known it was just another business deal.' The jibe was not lost on him.

'The accounts department is always happier if I entertain a group. I thought you'd feel safer with numbers. Amanda is not my girlfriend, by the way. Her father's a director of the company.'

'Perhaps you should tell her that. I've rarely seen such a display from someone who's just the boss's daughter.'

'Did you get my roses the other day?' She was thrown by the question and realised she had forgotten to phone Uncle Ted.

'Thank you, yes. I meant to phone Uncle Ted to say thank you. He must think me very rude and ungrateful.'

'He didn't know anything about them. My secretary organised it for me. Quite indispensable, a good secretary.'

Zara felt better. She would hate to hurt Uncle Ted, but as it had been a secretary's chore, it seemed less of a gaff.

'I don't feel so bad then. Do I thank you personally, or Asprey's or even your secretary?'

Oliver said nothing. He leaned across her and opened the car door.

'Goodnight, Zara. I had hoped you might invite me in for a coffee but you clearly dislike my company for some reason. We shall be friends eventually, I promise you. I can be very patient.'

She got out of the car, once more feeling angry with herself. This man had the power to make her feel very small, especially when he tried to compliment her.

'Goodnight,' she managed to mumble. 'And thank you for dinner. It was delicious.' She turned and almost ran into the safety of her flat. She did not wait for him to drive away and might have been disturbed if she had seen the expression on his face. The light blue eyes had set in a resolute, icy glare and the handsome face wore a look, partly puzzled, partly determined.

Zara arrived at the kitchen well

before anyone else the next morning and was hard at work by the time Lynne arrived.

'Either you haven't been to bed at all, or you've developed a passion for food. How was the evening, or shouldn't I ask?'

'It was OK. Surprising in some ways,' added Zara. Lynne's interest was aroused and Zara gave her a full account.

'Watch him, that's all I say,' Lynne warned. 'The sure fire way to catch you off guard, is to produce the other woman, preferably very glamorous. It's a well known strategy. He then makes you feel jealous, even if you're not, simply to try and prove what you are missing.'

'There speaks the happily married woman!' Zara laughed. 'You've become very cynical in your old age.'

'Must be my hormones. Pregnancy does funny things to you,' Lynne smiled. 'I'll put some coffee on. That's me, just the tea-girl. And to think I once had aspirations to be an executive. Where did I go wrong?'

Zara went back to her cooking. She always felt better doing something positive. Lynne was a super person to work with and she would be sorely missed when she stopped work to have her baby. When that happened, Zara would be kept very busy, with the cooking and organisation to look after.

At one o'clock, Zara took a tray into the office. It was loaded with a selection of savoury snacks, recipes that she'd been experimenting with during the morning. Garnished with salad, it looked most appetising.

'Wow,' Lynne exclaimed. 'Is this the executive treatment, after all? Lunch on a tray?'

'Thought you deserved a little treat and anyway, I thought we could decide on a few of these for inclusion in the menus. Strictly a working lunch, before you desert me entirely.'

Naturally, Lynne was looking forward to her baby's arrival, but was adamant about returning to work as soon as possible.

'If I stick to the office side, I should easily manage. Tony can do his share of baby minding at weekends and the odd evening, so I can play a full role.'

'As long as . . . ' Zara was interrupted by the telephone. 'I'll get it,' she offered. 'You finish eating. Hello? Gannets, Zara speaking.'

'Hi, Amanda here. We met last night. You do a bit of cooking, Oliver tells me?'

'Hello, Amanda,' Zara replied, intrigued. 'Yes, we provide catering for all occasions.'

'Good. I'm organising a party soon. At my parents' home. Send me some details of your menus, costs etc. Hope you can cope with large numbers.' The woman sounded thoroughly bored with life and extremely patronising, but she was a potential client. Zara managed to maintain her calm. She spoke professionally and quickly got a picture of what was required. She wrote down the details.

'Well, well,' Zara said, putting the phone down. 'Guess who that was?'

'There's only one person I know called Amanda. Perhaps the evening was worth it after all.' Lynne smiled ironically, as she spoke.

'Sounds like she's not short of money . . . wants the full works for her party, whatever it is in aid of. Just the sort of thing we need. Apparently half the County will be there. Twenty-sixth of this month.'

Lynne was delighted. Zara was troubled. She sensed there was something more to it . . . Amanda was devious. Zara couldn't help but suspect her motives in booking Gannets. Somehow, she felt it was planned to score a point and somehow Oliver was going to be involved. But Amanda was welcome to him. All the same, she knew she was trying to fool herself and that she did mind. She minded a lot.

'Asprey's have made another booking,' said Lynne later, bursting into the kitchen in great excitement. They specially asked for you to serve it. I guess our Oliver wants to see you again.

'Purely business, Lynne. That's all it is.'

'If you say so, love. Friday lunchtime. Twelve people. Menu number two. OK?'

'Excellent. I'll get on with it right away.' Zara was pleased to be busy again, with a definite purpose.

Friday came. She drove to the company with a sense of anticipation mingled with slight apprehension. She was beginning to mistrust her own feelings. Much to her relief, there was no sign of Oliver. She stepped back to look at her display and felt satisfied with her efforts.

'Lovely job, Miss,' said a voice behind her. She swung round to see Oliver, casually draped against the door.

'Good morning, Mr Pendlebury,' she said icily.

'Mr Pendlebury? I thought we might have progressed beyond the Mr stage?'

'It is more appropriate in the working environment,' she snapped back.

'Fine. If that makes you comfortable.' His eyes glinted. He could be patient. Zara had sensed his thoughts and was equally determined that she would never be just another of his conquests.

'Look,' he went on, 'suspend hostilities for a moment. I'd like you to come to a party. It might do you some good. The managing director is putting on a thing for the company . . . well for the senior staff. As a newcomer, I am supposed to be getting to know everyone on an informal level and it would be good to have you along. What do you say?' He was putting all his charm into this attempt to persuade her.

'I need to think about it. When is it?' she replied, stalling for time.

'Twenty-sixth of this month. It's a Saturday.'

'I'm sorry,' she said, realising she meant it, 'we have a booking. Big function . . . can't possibly get out of it.

51

Lynne, my partner, couldn't possibly manage alone.' She truly felt a mixture of relief and disappointment. She knew it was important to make contacts but she felt that everything was slightly out of control where Oliver Pendlebury was concerned. She hated this unsettled feeling he provoked in her.

'Shame,' said Oliver, looking as if he also meant it. 'Another time perhaps?'

'Perhaps,' she agreed. 'Now, the lunch party?'

Oliver left with no further comment. The clients arrived for lunch and Zara was kept busy serving and replenishing plates. She delighted in the compliments, doing her best to remember them to share with Lynne. When everyone had left and she was clearing the plates into their containers, Geoff, the security man, came through with a message.

'Mr Pendlebury phoned through to the desk. Said I was to ask you to call in at his office before you leave.'

As far as she could tell, everything

had gone well. There had been no complaints and someone had even asked for one of their cards. She frowned slightly, wondering what she was about to face this time. Something clicked in her mind. The big party Oliver had spoken of, she knew exactly who was doing the catering. Amanda was the boss's daughter, wasn't she?

4

Still seething, Zara tapped on the door of Oliver's office. She thought she'd heard him call come in and pushed it open. He was on the phone and gestured towards a seat opposite his desk.

'Fine, yes, I understand. I said yes. Look Amanda, I said yes. Now I need to get back to my work.' He put the phone down and looked furious. 'I'm sorry about that.'

'I'm sorry I interrupted. I thought you'd said come in.'

Oliver leaned back in his chair. He looked troubled and gave her a wan smile.

'Thanks for stopping by,' he began. She inclined her head. 'I think I now know why you can't accompany me to the party. Are you doing the catering?'

'Yes. Amanda called and booked us.

Sounds like quite a do. I couldn't refuse of course as we need the business and who knows what else could come out of it.'

'Just watch yourself. I suspect she might have ulterior motives. But, for your sake, I hope all goes well. I'm sure you're right. It could be good for you and there will certainly be lots of folk there who could well bring you more business.'

'Thanks for the support. Must say, she did give us something of a put down when she called. But always the professional. I trust everything was to your satisfaction today?'

'Fine thanks. Look, I'm sorry about earlier. I should have realised you would be doing Amanda's party. She'd already asked for your contact details so I should have guessed. I hope you won't find it awkward.'

'Of course not. Why should I?' He stared at her with his particularly inscrutable smile hovering round his mouth.

'I'd hoped . . . never mind. Don't let her bully you. And don't do her any favours. She'll undoubtedly try to do a deal with you, thinking she has some special case. The family are loaded so make sure you charge them the full price.'

Zara smiled. She had every intention of being totally professional about the deal. There was no way Amanda would get preferential treatment on the grounds of once sharing a dinner table. Gannets would give excellent service and charge a fair price.

'I assure you, Gannets is a fully professional company.'

'Zara,' he said softly. 'Zara, I . . . ' He hesitated and she took the chance to escape. The touch of his hand on her shoulder had produced a very strange sensation. She just knew he was trying to soften her up.

She must never allow herself to trust a man like this. She nodded at Oliver's secretary, Jenny as she passed her desk. How lovely Uncle Ted could be the father of someone like Oliver, she didn't know. She walked along the corridor towards the entrance foyer when she heard her name being called.

'Miss er . . . Zara, isn't it?' She turned to see Amanda standing in an office doorway. 'Oh, it is you. I gathered from what Oliver said that you were in the building. I thought we might discuss those menus. We need to make considerable changes to your rather basic ideas. A little provincial don't you think?'

'Amanda. Good afternoon.' Zara did not allow herself to respond the way her impulses were dictating but smiled sweetly. 'We are delighted to accommodate whatever you require for your party. If there is something particular you wanted, then please say. I sent you a range of menus for guidance only.'

'I was thinking more caviar than smoked salmon. Bit commonplace these days. I understand you can even buy it in supermarkets now.'

'Indeed. Makes it more available to

everyone, don't you think?' What a snob this woman was.

'I prefer exclusivity. Insist on it, actually. This is to be a very special occasion when Asprey's will show this part of the world exactly what we are about. Among other things of course. Celebrations ahead. So, you see, your little menu will need to be a lot more special if it is to serve its purpose.'

'Fine. And do you have a price per head in mind? A budget?'

'Whatever it takes. But as you cater in-house for our company, I trust there will be some sort of discount? After all, we are doing you a favour, a tiny new company trying to make a name for itself.'

As Zara's blood was reaching boiling point, she opened her mouth to tell this horrible woman exactly what she thought about her. A picture of Lynne, calm and serene and carrying her baby inside her came into her mind. She took a deep breath and forced a smile to her face.

'We may be a young business but I assure you, we already have an excellent reputation. If our prices are too high for you, then I suggest you find another company more suited to your requirements. I should warn you however, we won't be able to hold the date open for long. I suggest you let us know exactly how much you intend spending per head and any special additions, such as the caviar you mentioned and we will see how we might best accommodate you. Please excuse me now, I have another engagement.'

Angrily, she drove back to the kitchen and poured out her indignation to the ever patient Lynne.

'At least you managed to keep your temper. And people with that sort of attitude are probably too thick skinned to take offence at mild sarcasm. So, however shall we incorporate caviar into this menu? Horrible over rated stuff and fiendishly expensive. Should we buy a tin and experiment?'

'No way. I wouldn't be at all

surprised if they cancel the order anyway. We're far too provincial for the likes of Amanda and Oliver. No, we'll use it as a garnish on some of the prawn biscuit things we do. I don't intend to spend much time working on the ideas at this stage. Let her come back to us with some sort of budget and suggestions apart from caviar. Bloomin' snob.'

'I sense there may be some bread rolls coming up. Go and thump some dough. It usually helps you. And anyway, we need some of those olive and sundried tomato things you do, ready for next week. Plenty of space in the freezer.'

★ ★ ★

It was early the following week when Amanda's revised menu arrived in the post. She had chosen one of their cheapest menus and added several other items, which would exactly double the cost. Zara actually laughed aloud when she read the flamboyant

60

scrawl. Lynne read it and began calculating accurately what it would cost. After a few minutes, she picked up the phone and dialled the number on the headed notepaper.

'Ms Asprey? Gannets calling. Lynne speaking. Thank you for your letter this morning. We can certainly provide everything on your list but I should advise you that the cost of your special additions will bring it up to double our original suggested quote. This is of course including a ten percent discount, as the company is now a regular client. Perhaps you will consider this carefully and let us know your decision by the end of the day. Thank you.' Quietly, she put the phone down. Zara stared open-mouthed. Lynne smiled sweetly. 'I thought you might lose your temper if you did it.'

'And a ten percent discount? Can we afford it?'

'Certainly not, but I was suggesting a price that might look as if it could include that. Didn't give her time to comment, as you noticed. She'll probably try a few more companies but she won't do any better with that menu, even if she can find anyone to do it in the time. Must say we'll actually be pushed ourselves. It's not very long before the event.'

They began work, Lynne tackling the lighter jobs while Zara prepared a stack of vegetables for a party of vegans later in the week. The order was for curry and assorted side dishes.

'Can you just check all these various spices to make sure they're all suitable for vegans?' she asked Lynne. 'I'd hate to ruin our reputation by using the wrong thing. Vegetarian food is simple but for strict vegans, all sorts of innocent looking stuff can contain dairy produce or something else that's forbidden.'

They worked hard for most of the day, preparing, storing, freezing various things. Their investment in a fast freezing unit had been a godsend and made it possible to cook in advance and comply with food safety rules. At last, it was time to relax.

'We didn't hear back from Amanda. She must have found someone else. Shame, but I refuse to compromise on standards to give her a cheaper than viable buffet.'

'Absolutely right,' Zara agreed. 'We haven't got to face Oliver again this week, either. In fact, we're now a bit short of orders aren't we? Do you think we need another advert in the local press?'

'Not sure. But one idea you had was to supply puddings to local pubs. We could certainly follow up on that idea. How about cooking a few samples tomorrow and then taking them round to some local places to see reactions?'

By lunchtime the following day, an array of miniature cakes, gateaux and various other desserts in glass dishes, were set out on the main work surface. Zara called Lynne from the office.

'Wow,' she exclaimed. 'What a brilliant idea to do them as individual portions. They look gorgeous.'

'I thought I might photograph them and make some brochures. We could then do a mail shot with prices etc and thus save ourselves a lot of travelling.'

'Great. I'll happily sit and play with some ideas on the computer. We should get them printed professionally. I know it will cost a bit but I think it would be well worth it. We can include them with any of our menus when we send them out. That's terrific, Zara. Well done.'

They gave each other a hug. It wasn't easy with Lynne's bump. 'There's the phone. Back to work, you. You collect the orders and tell me what to cook next.'

While Lynne was dealing with the call, she set out a pretty cloth to set off her photographs. She brought in a spotlight and fiddled around getting everything just right before taking her pictures. With her digital camera, it was easy to take a great many shots and choose the best ones for printing. Lynne came back from the office.

'Guess what? Amanda has finally placed her order. Price and menu agreed. We have two and a half weeks to cook up the party food of a lifetime. This could be a huge deal for us. As you said it looks as though half the County will be there and if we do it well, it could be the start of something really big. I'll make a start on the lists of ingredients and get the ordering under-way. Any of those calorie laden puds going begging?'

'Help yourself, love. And well done. I suspect we're on our way. But don't get lulled into a false sense of security. This isn't going to be an easy one.'

⋆   ⋆   ⋆

On her way home that evening, Zara called in on her father with a couple of the samples. As always, he was delighted to see his daughter and settled her down with an end-of-day glass of wine. She told him about the forthcoming party.

'It should mean, if all goes as planned that we can pay back your loan. I think there could be several more orders coming out of it too, assuming all goes well.'

'You're not to worry about the loan. If I need, I'll come back to you. But you need to keep some cash flow available. Now, tell me more about this party of yours. Is it the Asprey's directors' do?'

'Well yes, I suppose so. Though Amanda Asprey is treating it as her own personal event. How do you know about it?'

'Ted invited me. He's been asked as Oliver's father and a retired employee anyway. An old friend of Tom Asprey too. They go back to the early days. Ted thought he'd like me as his guest. The invite was for two anyway. Not really my sort of thing but well, it's a bit of a favour for an old friend. At least I know the food will be superb.'

'Aw, thanks Dad. It'll be nice to have at least one or two friendly faces there. Make up for the snooty Amanda.'

'And what about Oliver? Isn't he a friendly face? I gather he took you out to dinner. Ted seemed very pleased about that.'

She explained about the reality of the meal and tried to make sure her father knew the exact situation between them. No way could she ever fall for him, however happy it might make their parents.

'I don't know what it is about him but I feel I can't trust him. He's not exactly Mister Bad Guy, but he manages to set my teeth on edge somehow. He's attractive in his way I suppose, but certainly not my type.'

Zara spent the evening sorting out new recipes and working out quantities for the party. She had brought the folders home to make sure Lynne had a proper rest. Her friend was always working as hard as she could and it wasn't sensible with the approach of the baby. This was a way she could take away more of the workload. At ten o'clock she felt weary enough to go to bed. What a life, she sighed.

Actually going out to have fun seemed to have disappeared entirely from her life lately. Even weekends were mostly spent catering for some function or other and exhaustion usually set in as soon as she arrived back at her flat. Still, once the business was fully operational, they might take on more staff and she could once more think about a social life. Even Richard, Oliver's friend, had never called back to invite her on the promised sailing trip . . . not that she particularly wanted to go but it would have been nice to be asked. She was certainly out of the social circuit these days.

With several smaller orders to fill and their regular weekly buffets, the two girls were working flat out. Lynne was looking very pale and weary and Zara insisted she left the kitchen early each evening. It meant she was working late most days but it didn't matter to her. She went home and almost fell into bed, slept solidly till it was time to get up the following day to make an early start.

With one hundred and fifty guests to cater for, this was one of their biggest orders so far. It was not helped by Amanda's twice daily phone calls to check on some detail or other and demand something special in the way of table décor.

Flowers of a particular colour and napkins that were impossible to find. The final bombshell hit them two days before the event. Evidently, Amanda was expecting them to provide bar staff. Champagne was being imported directly from a contact in France and Gannets was expected to provide people to serve it.

'I trust she's got glasses organised?' Zara said suddenly.

'Oh heavens, I'd better ask I suppose,' said the harassed Lynne. She came back into the kitchen moments later, looking quite white. 'No. She expected we'd be able to provide them as well.'

'OK. Time to call on my dad. He said to let him know if he could help at all. He can do the champagne glass search for us. And I'd better see if we can rustle up some bar staff. Maybe some of the *Mums* have husbands who could help. I wonder what else that woman has up her sleeve? She clearly wants us to fail. Though why she should, I don't know. It's her party that could be ruined, after all.'

Lynne insisted on staying till after seven on the Friday evening before the party. Despite Zara's pleas for her to go and rest, she was still working to the last minute.

'I'm fine. I'm not leaving everything to you. You've been working late every night this week and it isn't fair. We're a team.'

'Of course we are, but you have the baby to think of. Mike would never forgive me if I put that little one in danger. Oh, is he still OK to take charge of the barmen tomorrow?'

'Fine. He's pleased to be involved

and says he can keep an eye on me this way. I had to tell him he'd be far too busy for that. I've got a couple more husbands of the waitress team lined up by the way. That's five altogether. They should manage, don't you think?'

'Yes, but Madam will have to pay extra. They were certainly not included in the original quote. You know, I think we're about finished here for tonight. Now, clear off home. You look shattered. I'll finish the washing up and get home myself. Give me a hug. And well done us. Don't you agree?'

'See you in the morning. Have a good sleep.'

'I will. And you.'

As she wandered round their immaculate kitchen, Zara smiled happily. Their dream was coming true. This party was their biggest event so far and was surely going to lead to many more big occasions. Society weddings. Garden parties. There was no limit. They might have to expand

and even move to larger premises. They'd show the stuck up Amanda what they were made of and Oliver could smile his patronising smile on the other side of his face.

5

The early sun heralded a bright, warm day. 'At least it isn't raining for us when we have to carry all our stuff into the house,' Lynne said gratefully.

'I think the heat might be more of a problem. Our chilled van isn't that large and the fridges at the Aspreys' house will all be full of champagne. I hadn't really thought through the fact that it could be so hot.'

'Hadn't thought of that. What on earth shall we do?'

'There's a large wine chiller in the Asprey's headquarters. It's very close to their house. Maybe we can get it over there. That means we'd have some more fridge space at least. We daren't risk food poisoning. That would finish us off forever. Shall I call Oliver and see if he can organise to do it for us?'

'Is that all right? I mean, knowing

how you feel about him.'

'This is for Gannets. I shall swallow my pride for the company. Hope he's at home. If not, I can always get Uncle Ted to do the dirty work on my behalf.' She dialled the number.

'Oliver Pendlebury,' said the curt voice.

'Oliver. It's Zara. We have a problem and I'm hoping you can help us out.'

'I'm a lousy cook.'

'Nothing like that. It's just that it's such a hot day and likely to stay that way. We are really pressed for cold space. I wonder if it might be at all possible to borrow the Asprey's wine cooler? Amanda's got champagne filling their fridges and our van isn't large enough to hold everything that needs to be kept cold.'

'Leave it to me. I'll see what I can do. I'll see if I can get Geoff to deliver it later on this morning.'

'Thank you so much. I'm sorry to trouble you.'

'No bother. And I'll see if he can get

the large kitchen fridge moved over too. It's completely empty and works all right. If we do it early and carefully, it shouldn't be a problem.'

'You're a star. Thanks, Oliver.'

'My pleasure. Perhaps you'll think of me as less of an ogre in future. I shall look forward to having a drink or even a dance with you this evening. I gather your father is keeping mine company.'

'Yes, that's right. But I shall have to decline the drink. I shall be working flat out if I'm to satisfy Her Majesty. Oh, I'm so sorry. How rude of me. It just slipped out.'

'I can imagine exactly why you call her that. Quite a lady, our Amanda. I'll see you later.'

'Thanks again, Oliver. We're most grateful.' She put the phone down.

Zara took the first load over to the Aspreys' house while Lynne organised the work at the kitchen. She had a couple of the helpers meeting her there and they began to arrange tables and set out serving dishes ready for the food. Oliver came into the large dining room and went over to Zara.

For a moment, she hesitated, almost failing to recognise him. He hadn't shaved and his dark stubble made him look quite different. His pale blue eyes seemed accentuated and she realised he actually had the longest lashes she'd ever seen on a man.

'Hi, you. I've put the wine cooler near the back door and the other fridge in the kitchen itself. Anything else I can do?'

'That's great. Thank you so much. I don't know why we didn't think of it earlier. I suppose this is going to be one of the hottest days of the year so far. Nice for Amanda, though. It will make a much nicer evening if we can be outside.'

'Darling,' Amanda's voice rang out. 'I didn't know you were coming over this morning.' She crossed to Oliver's side and planted a kiss on his cheek. She would have kissed his mouth but he turned away. 'My, my, not your usual immaculate self yet, are we? I admit though, I quite like the designer stubble. Little harsh on the cheek maybe.'

'I'm saving getting smart till later.'

'So why are you here?'

'Just making sure the wine cooler arrived safely.'

'Oliver to the rescue once more. I didn't realise you weren't providing one of your own,' she sneered at Zara.

'You didn't actually ask for it when you placed your order, rather late in the day. As I said at the time, we needed to know in advance exactly what you were expecting. But I think we've managed to pull out the stops and fill all the additions to your original booking. But that particular problem seems to have been solved now. Please excuse me, I must get on.'

The guests were invited for six-thirty with drinks and savouries in the garden, where music was to be played by a local string quartet. The buffet supper was to be served at eight, followed by dancing for those who wanted to join in.

Amanda spent the entire day touching things and tweaking cloths and napkins. She had several tantrums when she decided the flowers and napkins weren't exactly the shade she had expected. It was almost time for the first guests to arrive when Amanda's father, Tom Asprey, put in an appearance. He looked at the tables and peered into the fridge to see the food.

'My goodness, what a wonderful display. I've been hearing such good things about you. Reports of your excellent lunches have come back to me. Well done. And I gather you and Oliver are old friends?'

'Well, hardly. Our parents were old friends. Oliver and I have scarcely ever met up again till recently.'

'We're very impressed with him, here at Asprey's. In fact, this evening is largely about introducing him to everyone. Our guest of honour.'

'Does he realise that? I mean, he . . . well . . . he never mentioned it.' She had been about to say he had asked her to accompany him but thought this may not have been quite the right thing.

'Maybe he doesn't. I believe Amanda has also been planning a short speech. Mercifully short, I hope. I look forward to sampling this delicious looking spread. Well done.'

'Thank you. I hope you have an enjoyable evening.' What a charming man. How could he possibly be the father to such a daughter as Amanda? Zara turned away and went to look for Lynne. The *Mums* were arriving for waitress duty.

By eight o'clock, everything was moved from the fridges to be ready on the buffet table. It was a splendid spread. The cocktail savouries had all gone down really well and the *Mums* were reporting back with enthusiastic comments. Zara noticed that the only things left uneaten were the caviar snacks. She smiled. Had Amanda noticed? She hoped so. It was still hot and there were several small tables left outside for anyone who preferred to sit out where it was a little cooler.

She looked around for Lynne. She heard the compliments on many lips as she walked round, looking for her partner.

'I say, you have done a superb job,' said one of the men she recognised from the lunch parties. 'You must give me your card. We have our silver wedding coming up later in the year. Be nice to surprise my wife.'

'Thank you. Thank you very much. If I don't catch up with you later, I'll leave some cards with the reception at Asprey's. You can pick one up from there.' She overheard Amanda talking to another woman.

'Yes, not a bad spread. Of course I had to intervene. I think we'd have been eating steak pies otherwise. Not much imagination there. But they're quite adequate little cooks on the whole. And at least they are capable of following orders. That alone makes it worth booking them.'

Angrily, Zara turned away. She felt quite capable of murder at that moment. Adequate little cooks indeed! Now where was Lynne? She looked into the kitchen. Her friend was sitting on a chair, holding her stomach. She was as white as a sheet.

'Lynne? Are you all right? You look dreadful. Oh lord, I knew it was too much for you. I'll get Mike.'

She rushed off towards the drinks table. 'Mike. You need to come to the kitchen. It's Lynne. She looks terrible and I really don't think she's well. I hope the baby's all right. I knew she shouldn't be overdoing things the way she has been.'

Mike rushed to his wife's side. He took one look at her and pulled out his mobile to call an ambulance.

'I'm not taking any risks. You're going to hospital immediately,' he told Lynne. 'And don't start saying you'll be all right in a minute. Now, don't look like that, Zara. It isn't your fault. You just carry on with everything and

I'll try to go as inconspicuously as possible. Go on with you. Make sure my lads are all coping without me. Go on now. I'll let you know how things are later.'

Looking very shaken herself, Zara went back to the party and checked everything was going smoothly. There was a call to charge glasses so everyone was busy refilling and shushing each other. It was time for the big speech. Tom Asprey, looking extremely relaxed and smart in his black tie chinked his glass for silence.

'Welcome, everyone. I hope you have enjoyed the excellent food provided by Gannets. Zara, come and take a bow on behalf of your company. Excellent service we've all had too.'

She blushed at the unexpected tribute and moved forward with a slight nod of the head. There was applause and murmurs of appreciation.

She caught a glimpse of Oliver standing with his and her fathers and saw them all beaming with pleasure.

Amanda on the other hand, was scowling. She wanted all the credit and was clearly displeased with her father for singling out Zara for any compliments. Tom continued.

'You are all here tonight to meet the latest addition to our team. We are delighted to welcome Oliver Pendlebury as a senior member of our board. He may be our youngest senior manager but I'm sure he is making quite an impact already.'

There was a ripple of applause. Oliver himself stepped forward looking even more uncomfortable than she had felt herself. There were calls of *speech, speech*. He began.

'I'm sorry, but I was not expecting to be asked to speak here tonight. Nor was I aware till now that this was a party to welcome me to Asprey's. But, thank you. Thank you, Tom, for such a glowing introduction. I hope I can fulfil everything he hopes for and look forward to working with you all. Well, those of you who do actually work here.

I can see there are a number of friends and family also in attendance tonight and I look forward to knowing all of you in time. I hope to have a long and happy association with you all.'

Amanda stepped forwards and linked her arm into Oliver's. She leaned against him provocatively and took the microphone from him.

'I'd also like to add a few words about Oliver. We haven't known each other for very long but for both of us, it has been something of a whirlwind romance. He is too modest to tell you himself, but not only has he joined my father's company, but he is also joining our family. Oliver and I are to be engaged to be married.'

She leaned towards him again and kissed him on the lips, as the crowd clapped and cheered. Zara felt the room swaying slightly. Though she had declared she wasn't interested in him, the idea of his marrying Amanda was almost too much. Why on earth hadn't he warned her? She moved away and found herself near to her father and Uncle Ted.

'What a surprise,' she mumbled. 'You must be delighted.'

'Surprised, yes. Very. Disappointed though. She doesn't seem to me to be his type of lady at all. I had no idea myself. And judging from the look on Oliver's face, he had no idea either.'

'No. Really? You mean this is just Amanda trying to cause a sensation? But she's always seemed very close to Oliver.' She thought about the few times she had seen them together. Amanda had always been very pushy and it was usually her making the gestures. In fact, most of the time, Oliver had looked positively uncomfortable.

'I foresee taxing times ahead,' Uncle Ted said gravely. 'Oliver is not a man to be propelled into anything he doesn't want but it could make his future with the company somewhat difficult.'

'Perhaps he has decided to go ahead with this to ensure progress in his work.

High price to pay though.'

'Too high. Not something he would be likely to do either. Not my Oliver.'

The little group watched as Amanda dragged her prize around the room, shaking hands with everyone and accepting congratulations. From somewhere, she had even managed to attach a ring to her finger. It was a large emerald, surrounded by diamonds and was one of the most beautiful things Zara had ever seen.

She suddenly felt very weary and not a little sad. Though she knew she didn't ever intend to be close to Oliver herself, he really deserved someone nicer than the horrid Amanda. Her father stood close to her and put a hand on her shoulder.

'Never mind, darling. You said you couldn't love the bad guy and now it looks as if he's got what he deserved.'

'Thanks, Dad. I'm so glad you're here tonight. But, I'm supposed to be working so I'd better go and work. I need to know what's happening with

Lynne as well.' She went back to the kitchen and started to organise the crates of dirty dishes. They would all be washed in the machine back at the kitchen and then returned to the hire company on Monday morning.

It would be nice when they could afford to buy their own plates and dishes. A few more events like this one and it wouldn't be so far away. Perhaps Gannets could do the catering for Amanda and Oliver's wedding. She shuddered at the prospect.

'Zara. Please stop. We need to talk.' It was Oliver. She wished the ground would open beneath her feet.

'Really? Congratulations, by the way. I doubt there's much to say, actually. It would have been nice to be told about this . . . this engagement. And to think, you actually asked me to accompany you to the party. How embarrassing would that have been?'

'I assure you, it was probably more of a shock to me than anyone else. I never, ever gave her grounds to think I'd be remotely interested in her. As for getting married to her, she is the last person in the world I'd marry. I'm only still here so her father isn't embarrassed by my denials. He's much too nice a man to be compromised. She's the most awful woman I've ever met.'

'Why don't I believe you?'

'What more can I say? I knew nothing about it.'

'Right. And I suppose she had the engagement ring in her pocket, all ready for the big event?'

'Exactly. Some old family heirloom, I gather.'

'Well, I hope you'll both be very happy. Excuse me now. I have work to do.'

'Zara,' he called but it was too late. She had gone back into the kitchen.

Zara's mobile beeped to announce the arrival of a text message.

Lynne and baby fine and still in place. Keeping her in for a few days. Says she's sorry to let you down, Mike.

It was midnight by the time she took

the first load of stuff back to the kitchen. She was almost asleep on her feet and couldn't face unpacking things that night. She would probably need to make a number of trips back and forth to Asprey's tomorrow so it would be another busy day and all without Lynne's support.

She plonked down the last crate and switched off the lights. She needed to rest now. If this company of theirs was going to be successful, they needed contingency plans. Relying on just two of them with casual help wasn't going to work.

Zara slept heavily and woke much later than she had planned. She took the time to cook a proper breakfast and sat quietly enjoying scrambled eggs and bacon as she went over the events of the previous day.

The whole thing had been a great success . . . a triumph, but Amanda's announcement had spoilt everything for her. There was no logic to her thoughts as she had firmly discounted any chance of her and Oliver being more than colleagues.

But she held such dislike for that woman, she realised she even begrudged her being happy. What a nasty person she must be. She went for a shower and tried to wash away her nasty thoughts.

She stopped at the kitchen and put a load into the dishwasher. The place looked as if a bomb had hit it and it was going to be a long day. She collected the Gannets' van and drove over to Asprey's large house.

There were several cars parked outside, including Oliver's. She drove round to the back and began to tackle the debris left in the kitchen.

Once everything belonging to Gannets was removed, she would need to clean the kitchen. It was almost too much to face on her own.

'Hey, thought you could do with some help,' said a voice.

'Oh Mike, how wonderful to see you. But shouldn't you be with Lynne? How is she?'

'She's fine. Nagged me to come and help in her place. I gather this lot needs taking out to the van? I can load up my car too so it will save a few trips.'

'Thanks so much. I was wondering how on earth I'd manage.' She carried a load of things out to the van and went back inside. Coming down the imposing stairway was Oliver.

'Need some help?' he said. Zara's heart turned over.

'Of course not. You're a guest. I couldn't possibly ask you to do anything.'

'Nonsense. I have nothing else to do this morning.'

'Really? And is Amanda happy with that?'

'Nothing to do with me. As I said, the whole business was her idea and I knew nothing about it.'

'Darling,' Amanda's strident voice drifted down from above. 'I'm in dire need of lots of coffee. After last night, can you blame me? What about you, darling? Nice breakfast to replenish your energy? I'm sure Zara won't mind putting a cosy breakfast together for us? We'll use the small breakfast room. You'll find eggs and all the stuff in the fridge.'

Zara thought her blood would boil. A feeling of cold anger swept through her entire body and she felt as if she might fall over. For once her renowned red-hair temper flared uncontrollably.

'I'm sorry, Amanda, but I'm here to clear up. If you want your breakfast cooked for you, you need to engage a permanent cook. Excuse me.' She went into the kitchen and began tossing things into boxes with total lack of care.

'Steady on. What's wrong?' Mike asked.

'It's all right. I'm just very angry. That woman. She only expects me to cook breakfast for her and Oliver. Right. If you could put this lot into the van, I'll start cleaning the surfaces and scrubbing the floor.'

As they were leaving Tom Asprey came outside to speak to them.

'Thank you again for everything.

You've left the place spotless. Let me have your bill on Monday morning and I'll make sure we pay in full immediately.'

'Thank you. I appreciate that. It will be somewhat higher than the quote, as we had to engage bar staff. Amanda hadn't included that in her original request.'

'No problem. You really did us proud. The only criticism I'd make, if you don't mind my saying it. Those savouries with caviar. Rather pretentious don't you think? The biscuit things were delicious but not many people actually appreciated the caviar. Very much an acquired taste, especially as it was such a hot day.'

'I do agree. I doubt we'll ever do them again anyhow but your daughter was adamant.'

'I bet she was. All very strange this engagement thing too. Did you know anything about it? Never breathed a word of it to me before the announcement. Delighted of course. Oliver's a fine young man and I couldn't wish for a better son-in-law. But between ourselves, didn't you think he looked a little surprised, too? Well, maybe. But they have been seeing quite a lot of each other.'

'Really? I wasn't aware.'

'But, I mustn't keep you. I expect you have a lot to do. Oh and I hope your partner is all right. Let me know how she gets on, won't you? Thanks again. Splendid. All quite splendid.'

She drove back to their kitchen to meet Mike, smiling as she went. What a really nice man was Tom Asprey. Mike was already unloading more boxes and crates and beginning to organise the mess.

'I've got another hour before I need to go and see Lynne. What would you like me to do?'

Gradually, they worked through the washing up and packing hired dishes back into their crates. Mike loaded them straight into the van, ready to take back the next day. The commercial dishwashing machine was wonderfully quick and order was rapidly being restored.

'Oh Mike, thank you so much. It was certainly much less daunting with two of us. I think I'd have been in tears by now, left on my own.' Mike left for the hospital and she continued her work. There was a knock at the door and she went to answer it, surprised that anyone would be around on a Sunday after-noon. Oliver stood there with a large pizza box.

'Thought you might have forgotten to eat, I never saw you eating anything yesterday and you'll be collapsing. Besides, I was starving myself today. No breakfast this morning.' He had a wicked glint in his eyes as he spoke.

'And all that energy you needed to replenish.' She couldn't help herself.

'Amanda's fantasy yet again. How many times can I tell you? It's all her imagination. In her mind. She's the last person I'd ever marry. If I ever thought of getting married at all. Now, pizza?'

Zara's stomach rumbled as the smell of the hot savoury food escaped from the box.

'I admit to being famished. Clear a space on the top there. I'll look for a clean plate and knife and fork.'

'Fingers will do for me.'

The food tasted wonderful and they both ate greedily. Greasy fingers were wiped and Zara relaxed for the first time in days.

'Just what I needed,' she said gratefully. 'But now, it's back to work.'

'And I'm here to help for the rest of the afternoon.'

Oliver was as good as his word. His mobile rang several times but he ignored it. Amanda, she assumed, trying to discover where he was. By four-thirty, everything was looking neat and tidy and all surfaces cleared and cleaned.

'Thank you very much for your help. I do appreciate it but I need to go and see Lynne in hospital now. I'm sure you need to get back to your fiancée. I doubt she'll be very pleased if she knows where you are. She'll see it as a further sign that Gannets can't cope.'

'I don't care what she thinks. You have proved yourselves and I hope there's plenty more business coming along. Zara, I wish you'd believe me. Give me a chance.' He took her hand and pulled her towards him. He kissed her lips and she felt herself responding. Then she pushed him away.

'No. Oliver, no. Go back to Amanda. She's your future.' He raised his hands helplessly in defeat, turned and went out to his car.

6

Zara repaired her make-up and drove to the hospital, Lynne was sitting up in bed, looking fresh and relaxed. Mike was beside her, holding her hand.

'I'm so sorry,' she began. 'Leaving you in the lurch like that. How did it all go in the end?'

Zara gave her the details and said how brilliant Mike had been in helping.

'I wonder if we shouldn't offer him a job,' she laughed. 'Hope this doesn't mean you don't need me any more?' Lynne said with a frown. 'You seem to have managed everything without me.'

'Couldn't do it too often, love. Besides, I did have some help. Oh, and Tom Asprey asked after you. Wanted to know how you are. You're certainly being missed all round. So just you get yourself right again and get yourself back to that computer screen.'

'Would it help if I drove the stuff back to the hire company tomorrow?' Mike offered.

'If you're sure. That would be terrific. I am hoping we'll get some calls tomorrow. Several people asked for our cards. I put some in my pocket in the end and handed out quite a few. Maybe there will be masses of new orders pouring in. Now, tell me what they've said about you?'

'I'm fine. Just been overdoing things a bit. I have to take a couple of hours rest in the afternoons. Thought I might introduce a sofa to our rest room area. If that's OK with you.'

'I think you should go home in the afternoons, just for a few weeks. You've got less than two months to go. I was thinking we might take on an extra person anyway. One of the *Mums* or maybe two of them might like a job to share.'

★　★　★

When she got home, Zara put the television on and opened a bottle of wine. She had just slumped down in front of an antiques programme when her phone rang.

'Zara? It's Richard. Oliver's friend. I promised you I'd call and arrange a sailing trip. Sorry it took me so long but the boat's been out of the water and I'd also lost your phone number. Feeble, aren't I?'

'Richard, nice to hear from you,' she murmured politely.

'So how are you fixed for next weekend? I thought Saturday would be good, but Sunday would be OK if you're busy.'

'I . . . I need to look at our diary. We do often have bookings at weekends and I simply can't remember off-hand what's been booked.'

'OK. I hope yesterday went well? Oliver mentioned it was the big Asprey's shindig.'

'It was fine. A lot of hard work but they seemed pleased. Have you spoken to Oliver today?'

'Nope.'

'Oh, so you haven't heard the big news. He and Amanda are engaged.' She swallowed hard to stifle the lump of something that seemed to be rising in her throat.

'What?' Richard almost shouted. 'But he can't stand the woman. Surely not. Surely he isn't doing the promotion thing? The marry the boss's daughter routine. Not Oliver.'

'I'm not sure why it all happened but she made the announcement at the party last night. Ring and all. Whatever he says, it's definitely happening.' How much she wanted to hear denials. 'Look, can I call you when I've checked my diary. If I'm free, I'd love to come out with you. My partner's unwell at present so the business will be all down to me for a while.'

'I'm in shock. I must call the man himself. I'll give you my number and please make sure you call back. I'd love to see you again.' He gave her his number and she wrote it down. It might be something to look forward to, even if Richard wasn't the man she'd most like to be with.

Feeling rather depressed the next morning, she drove to the kitchen. Her first priority was to get the account sorted for the party and then, there was nothing for it but to deliver it by hand. Tom Asprey had said as much.

It would be good to have the money safely in the bank. Lynne had kept careful records of everything so it would be a simple matter to produce the statement and invoice. She switched on the computer and began to work. Easy, she thought as she printed out the final bill. Then she realised she hadn't added the extras. She began again as the phone rang.

Mike arrived and drove the van back to the crockery hire company, as Zara continued to answer telephone enquiries. By midday, she had a list of twelve people needing menus to be sent out and still an incomplete invoice for

Asprey's. It was terrific news but goodness, how long it might be before Lynne was back.

'I'm not sure she should really come back before the baby's born. She really needs to rest,' said Mike.

'I think I'd better try to get someone in here if only to man the phones. It's been ringing solidly all morning and I still haven't finished the invoice.'

She grabbed a quick snack and drove over to Asprey's headquarters. She hoped Tom himself would be there and that she could avoid meeting Oliver and especially Amanda. Geoff, the security man greeted her arrival.

'I gather there was quite a do on Saturday. I fetched the fridge and wine cooler back this morning. Everyone was saying how much they'd enjoyed it. And I heard about the big announcement. Quite a surprise for everyone.' Zara tried her best to smile.

'Yes, we were all surprised. I hope they'll be very happy.'

'They're in her office as we speak.'

'Actually It's Mr Tom Asprey I wanted to see. Is he available?'

'I'll see. Is he expecting you?'

'Maybe. He did say to bring in our invoice today. He suggested I should deliver it personally.'

Geoff dialled the number and spoke briefly to Tom's assistant.

'He'll see you in fifteen minutes. Do you want to wait here?' She nodded and went to sit in the waiting area. She heard raised voices coming from one of the offices. She glanced at Geoff who raised his eyebrows and gave a wry grin. A door banged along the corridor and Oliver stormed out. He crossed reception and saw Zara. He stopped in his tracks.

'Would you come to my office, please?' he asked.

'I'm waiting to see Mr Asprey, actually.'

'Buzz my office when he's ready will you, Geoff? Zara will be with me till then.' Unwillingly, she rose to her feet and followed him.

'I don't think we have anything to say, Oliver.'

'I have plenty to say. That damned woman. She's trying to organise my every move.'

'Amanda?'

'Who else. She's only put engagement announcements in all the major newspapers. How do I get out of this one? Help me, Zara.'

'Me? I can't. She's a determined lady. Knows what she wants and goes all out for it.'

'But I never gave her any encouragement. I've never even asked her to go out with me. She just pushed and pushed at every opportunity. That dinner we had. Invited herself along. That was why I asked Richard. She's always got her own way I gather. Twists her father round her little finger and he gives in to her.'

'No mother around?'

'I think she left them many years ago. I don't even know if she's still alive. We seem to have a bit of shortage of mothers between us all, don't we?'

Zara looked wan and bit her lip. She still missed her own mother, now three years since she had died.

'Oh, I'm so sorry. That was tactless of me. I'm so hyped up after the last encounter, I'm not thinking straight.'

'It's OK. But clearly, Amanda had lacked guidance from anyone. I suppose when you're heir to a huge company, you forget the need for tact. People are used to doing what you tell them.'

'Not this one. I will never do as I am told by the likes of her. What sort of life would it be? I'd have nothing left of myself. My inner self.' Zara was about to speak when the door burst open.

'Simply great news, darling. Daddy has agreed to make you his deputy. I know you're very young for such a position, but as I pointed out to him, he needs to give you a job commensurate with the status of his son-in-law. Oh, Zara, you're here again. Can't keep away from us, can you?' She walked round the desk and draped herself possessively over Oliver. 'We might even book your little organisation for the wedding. What do you think, darling?'

'I think you should go now. I was talking to Zara. A private conversation.'

'Surely there are no secrets between us now?' she said shyly.

'Mr Tom will see you now, Zara. Go straight up. Geoff will show you the way. Amanda, I have work to do. We'll talk later. Go away now, please.' The two women left his office together. Angrily, she grabbed Zara's arm, holding it far too tightly.

'I know exactly what you're trying to do. You won't succeed though. Oliver's mine and I don't intend losing him to some pathetic little cook insinuating her way in through tenuous family connections. Understand me? He'll do what I tell him or lose any chance of a future with this firm. He can't afford to lose the chances I can bring to him. He'll probably inherit the lot one day and I intend to be at his side when he does.'

'I assure you, Amanda, I am trying

nothing. I do not have any sort of agenda with Oliver. As far as I am concerned, he's yours for as long as you can hold on to him. Now, if you'll excuse me, I have a meeting with your father. Such a charming man.'

Seething with anger, Zara entered the director's suite. His personal assistant asked her name and showed her into the luxurious office. One side was entirely made of windows, overlooking the parkland. A huge oak desk was set to one side and a range of comfy leather seats was set at the other. Tom rose and came forward to greet her.

'Can I get you tea? Coffee?'

She shook her head as she declined. She might have spilled it all over everywhere, the way she was feeling. She took a deep breath to calm herself and forced a smile on to her face.

'Sit here, it's more comfortable.' She sank into the leather sofa and he sat beside her. 'Now, have you got your account ready for me?'

She handed him the envelope. 'It's

very kind of you to see me personally. I would have left it with reception, but you said . . . '

'Not at all. I wanted to speak to you. I left organising the contract with your company to someone else, but I do like to take a personal interest in everyone who works for us. As far as I can, of course. Trouble is, we're becoming such a huge organisation globally, I'm rapidly losing touch. But here at headquarters, I like to think I'm on the ball.'

'A wonderful ambition,' she said politely. 'One that must be next to impossible to achieve, especially if you see all the people out on the fringes, like me.'

'Can I ask you something personal?' She nodded. 'What do you know of Oliver Pendlebury? I'm a bit concerned about my daughter's infatuation with him. If that's what it is. She calls it love, but I somehow think she has underlying motives.'

'I can't possibly comment about that.

You'd have to ask her.'

'I'd like to speak frankly to you. My daughter's asked me to promote him. I'm not convinced he's ready for the job yet though. I suspect she's trying to offer bribes to keep him interested. What do you think?'

Zara gasped. What on earth was this man doing, asking her such personal questions? It seemed such an unlikely thing for anyone in his position to be doing and it certainly wasn't her place to give him any answers.

'Why ask me these things? It's between you and your daughter, isn't it?'

'I'm sorry. I shouldn't have embarrassed you. I understood there is some family connection between you. Ted Pendlebury is one of my oldest friends and I respect him tremendously. I'd love to see his son succeed but on his own merits. The trouble is, I've always spoiled my daughter. She's very headstrong and without a mother to guide her, I've, well I've given into her whims for the sake of an easy life. Dreadful admission isn't it?'

'I'm flattered that you should ask me for an opinion, but I couldn't give you an unbiased one. I do believe that she is trying to make it impossible for Oliver to leave her. She seems to be raising obstacles and putting tempting offers in his way. Whether or not he is happy about it all, I simply can't say.

'I do know he is alarmed by the speed of everything. He's only been here a short while and I think he was enjoying his new job very much. Now, if you will excuse me, I'd better get back to my office. I'm trying to manage single-handed at the moment.'

'One moment and I'll write you a cheque. This is on my personal account and the reason I wanted to deal with it myself. I'd like to do all our catering business with you, Zara. A new company is exactly what I like to promote, providing of course they are good enough. And you most certainly are.' He wrote the cheque and she slipped it into her bag without looking.

'Thank you very much, Mr Asprey. It's a treat to do business with someone who clearly cares about his company and his staff.'

'Tom. Please call me Tom. And I'm sorry again for trying to bend your ear. You were the soul of tact, my dear. I hope your partner, Lynne, is it? I hope she returns to work soon. We shall meet again soon, I'm sure.'

'Thank you Mr . . . Tom. Bye.'

As she walked down the corridor she was aware of Amanda watching her. She didn't turn or acknowledge that she had seen her and went straight out.

As she drove back to the kitchen, she turned over the various events of the afternoon. It was all very strange. Would Oliver really take the position that his so-called fiancée had organised? Perhaps his pride would stop him. What a schemer she was. It was going to be rather awkward working at the company and Tom had made it very clear that there would always be work with them. It was pretty much what Oliver had said.

They used the building for residential events and catering would be needed for such occasions. It was potentially a highly lucrative contract . . . if she could find some way of working with Amanda hovering around.

Back at the kitchen Zara noticed the answering machine was flashing madly. She took the cheque out of her bag. Tom had added an extra two hundred pounds to the total. After all Amanda's arguments about costs, her father had given them a bonus. It was great news and she was very touched at his generosity.

She scribbled a quick note of thanks on one of their cards and put it to one side to post. She pressed the play button on the answering machine and took out a pad to make notes.

Yet more enquiries about their services. They definitely needed to consider more staff. Gannets was on its way.

Once she had returned the call, it was too late to start any cooking. There wasn't much more she could do and she decided to leave early. That way she would have time to call and see Lynne at the hospital and tell her the good news. She picked up some flowers from the hospital shop and went to the maternity ward.

'Zara. How lovely to see you. Guess what? They're letting me out tomorrow. I have to promise to rest every afternoon but at least I can come and do the accounts and answer the phone. Isn't that great?'

'Certainly is. But I don't want you doing anything that might harm you or the Blob. Much better to take time-out now and be back in full swing when it's all over.'

'Mike's been getting to you, hasn't he? Don't you want me back then?'

'Course I do. In fact, I was going to suggest we get in a temp for a few weeks. The phone's never stopped ringing today. We've got heaps more bookings so I really do need to get some help. I thought of the *Mums*. One or two of them could do a job share. Oh and guess what? Tom Asprey gave us a two hundred pound bonus and that was on top of the extra for the bar staff and their baby sitters. Good, eh? And most of the new bookings are following the party so we certainly do owe them a lot.'

'And what of the great romance? Any news?'

'I'd rather not talk about it.'

'And you said you don't like Oliver. Hmm. I just don't believe you.'

'I was thinking of that woman. Poor Uncle Ted. She'll try to take over his life as well, you mark my words. And can you just imagine being related to her? Do you know the latest? She's trying to persuade her father to make Oliver his deputy. Hang on to him at all costs. Smacks of desperation to me.'

'Glad we're not talking about it.'

'What do you mean?'

'Nothing. Just think about what you

said and what you've talked about ever since.'

'Sorry, love. Tell me about you. What was the problem? What made you practically pass out on Saturday?'

'Good old blood pressure. I guess I was totally underestimating the stress of it all.'

'Every reason for you to stay away and let me get in some extra help.'

'No. I insist on coming in to do the admin. I can work sitting at the computer and you can wait on me hand and foot. Tasty, healthy snacks and drinks whenever I click my fingers.'

'Seriously, I'd be bored to tears with nothing to do and worrying about you coping all alone would send my blood pressure up to the roof. Besides, Gannets is half my company and I want to make sure it's flourishing. My child will need the best of everything and I intend to make sure she gets it.'

'Oh, so it's a girl, is it?'

'I just know it is. Well, I don't know really. We asked them to keep it a secret after the scan, but I just feel it's a girl.'

'So, what do you think?' Lynne asked.

'Sorry?'

'Thought you were day dreaming. You didn't hear a word, did you? Will you be godmother to the Blob?'

'Oh, Lynne, I'd be delighted. Thank you.'

Two days later, Lynne arrived soon after nine o'clock. She protested that she was being driven crazy with nothing to do and couldn't bear to think of Zara rushed off her feet. It was great to have her back and the pressure was off Zara, who no longer had to answer the phone all the time. It was a great relief. It was almost lunchtime when Lynne called her to the office.

'We have another lunch to do for Asprey's. Tuesday next week. Are you all right with it? I could do it if you really prefer not to go there.'

'No. Course I'll go. You are certainly not doing it. No way. I can smile sweetly at Her Majesty and make you proud of me. Oliver might be more of a problem, but I'll face that when I see him.'

'So, you finally admit you have feelings for him.'

'I guess so. Not much point now though, is there? He's well and truly hooked. Reeled in, netted and landed, to continue my fishing metaphor.'

'Some fish fall back into the pond though. Lines break and nets have holes in them.'

'I'll go and make some bread.'

7

Despite her brave words, it was certainly a strain to think of going to Asprey's again. Her last encounter with Amanda had been very unpleasant. She practically had the bruises on her arms to prove it. The conversation with Tom Asprey had also been most uncomfortable. But, it was an important job and she needed to be professional about it.

It was a simple menu this time. Individual portions of lasagne and a selection of salads with a couple of cold sweet choices. Evidently the sales conference merited less exotic fare. With Oliver nominally in charge of this department, he would undoubtedly be present. Having finally admitted to having feelings for him, she felt more nervous than ever.

On the Monday evening, she had a call from a slightly angry Richard.

'You promised to call me about the weekend? I assume you were working after all. But I kept it free for you, just in case.'

'I'm so sorry,' she replied. In truth, with all her other turmoils, she hadn't given the sailing invitation another thought. 'My business partner has been in hospital and I've been really stretched this week.' Bit of a lie but based on truth.

'I'm sorry to hear that. This next weekend's free if you are.'

'Thanks, Richard, but I think I'll have to take a rain check again. Life's just too complicated. Did you get hold of Oliver, by the way?'

'Did I just. Talk about the dragon getting her claws into him. She sounds a dreadful woman. You do know he doesn't want any of it?'

'He didn't seem to be protesting too much last thing I saw. And a great career opportunity.'

'I'm not sure what you heard. She threatened to get him the sack if he didn't play ball.'

'Really? I thought he was getting promotion.'

'Evidently not. Seems Daddy wouldn't agree. Big troubles over there, I'm telling you.'

'Oh dear. And I'm booked to do a meal there tomorrow. I'd better grow some thicker skin.'

'This was last week. It may have blown over by now. Anyway, nice to talk to you. I gather I'm never going to get that sailing date? Don't bother to answer that one. But, keep in touch and if you ever fancy a drink give me a call.'

'Thanks, Richard. And I'm sorry I didn't call you back. It was very rude of me. Bye.'

So, things were reaching a head were they? Tomorrow might be more interesting than she was expecting . . . or much more stressful.

Geoff greeted her as usual, from behind the reception desk.

'Nice to see you again. You're almost becoming part of the staff here, aren't you? Something nice today?'

'Hope so. Hot main course so I'd better get in there and set things up. See you later. Hope I'll have a little treat for you when I'm finished.'

'Lovely. Thanks, Zara. Miss Asprey will be through to see you sometime.'

'Great,' she said through gritted teeth. No doubt she would be delighted to have yet another gloat about her glorious future. She began work on setting up the meal. The old kitchen that had once been used for all the catering was still functional, though had been little used for some years. There were two rooms used for eating, with screens to separate them. If one larger room was needed, the screens could be opened out.

Today was for fifteen so she set about laying up the tables. The food was heating in the large oven, ready to be put on to the buffet table when needed. She hummed as she worked, absorbed in her task. She heard the door open and swung round, expecting to see

Oliver. She was disappointed.

'You haven't laid enough places. There are twenty in the party today.' Amanda looked smug at the thought of catching her out.

'You booked for fifteen. My colleague took the booking herself.'

'Let's hope you can feed everyone then.'

'You asked for individual portions. Fifteen of them. It doesn't lend to stretching it to twenty.'

'Your problem. Get it sorted. They'll be here in ten minutes.' Amanda swung out of the room and Zara grimaced. Once more the woman had tried to wrong foot her. She had actually brought over twenty portions. Admittedly, some of them were vegetarian but she didn't think that would matter at all.

They had learned it was essential to carry some veggie dishes these days. The salads would stretch and with a choice of dessert, there were extra of those too. Why Amanda always had to try to spoil everything, she didn't know. As the first of the sales team came into the room, she put the piping hot dishes on to the table and smiled at everyone. The whole time, she was looking out for Oliver but he didn't arrive. Tom himself came in and crossed the room to speak to her.

'Have you got a spare meal for me? I've had to come in and take the meeting. You do know Oliver has left us, I take it?'

'Of course there's enough food for you. Vegetarian or beef?' She could scarcely trust herself to speak. Oliver had gone?

'Oh how lovely. I'll try your vegetarian dish. Excellent. Good of you to cater for the special guests.'

'I didn't know Oliver had left. It must have been rather sudden.'

'Between you and me, I suspect it might have been a case of over-enthusiasm from my daughter. I decided he wasn't quite ready for the other job yet . . . the one we spoke of the other day. He seemed to have the idea that if he didn't take it, he would be out of the company for ever. But I was too late to stop him, he's gone to Australia, I understand. Anyway, enough of gossip. I'd better join my colleagues.' Zara stared after him. Evidently he wasn't quite the soft touch Amanda thought. But Australia? Surely she wasn't so bad that he had to go to the other side of the world? The woman herself came into the room.

'I'd like a portion of the . . . whatever it is.'

'Lasagne. Vegetarian or beef?'

'Oh there's a choice is there? Is everyone here?'

'I believe so. I had a few spares, as you will see. I'm not easily caught out,' Zara added. 'I hear Oliver has left.' She tried to see her ring finger, but Amanda kept it well hidden. She ignored Zara and took a portion of salad. If her heart was broken, it clearly wasn't affecting her appetite. Once everyone was eating, she cleared the serving table and put out the desserts.

'Well done again, Zara,' Tom said, as he was leaving. 'It was certainly a good day when we found you. I believe there's a residential weekend coming up. Will you cope with that? We have about twenty or so rooms for guests. You might prefer to stay over yourself. We have a company who come in to service the rooms so you wouldn't have any bother with that. We'd need meals. Breakfast. Buffet lunches and a dinner at night. How do you feel about that?'

'I'll put together a quote for you. I'll need to bring in extra staff of course. And the kitchen. Well, it really needs a good clean. It isn't up to standard at present and I'd have to do some preparation here. I doubt I could bring in enough ready prepared food from our own kitchen.'

'Fine. I'll organise it. Or get someone to do it.'

For a managing director, Tom Asprey seemed very hands on and involved with domestic details. She wondered why. Surely there were much more important things he should be doing? Still, not her problem. She spoke to her clients as they were leaving and accepted their thanks for the meal. Amanda of course did not speak and she left without a glance at her. Efficiently, Zara cleared everything away, loading it back on to her trolley and putting it away. She had only one pudding dish left and took it to Geoff.

'Sorry, but there were more people than were expected. This is the best I can do.'

'Very good of you to think of me at all. Hope you managed the extras. I saw her ladyship going your way. Expect it was her mess up. She specialises in causing chaos for all of us. Shame she insists on having an office here at all. Whoops, sorry. I'm speaking out of turn. I suppose you heard Mr Pendlebury's left us? Shame. He seemed such a nice man too. Miss Amanda must be heartbroken.'

'If she ever had one to break. Sorry, my turn to be nasty. Must go now. See you again soon.'

She poured out the news to Lynne, who was still at the office.

'Hey, you're supposed to be resting afternoons.'

'I am. I'm just sitting here with my feet up. So, it all went well. I'm sorry about Oliver but at least he's escaped from Delilah's clutches. That must be nice to know.'

'S'pose. Better get on with this quote. This is quite a big one for us. And you'll be right out of it probably giving birth or something equally mundane.'

'Cheek. So what shall we offer? And how many staff will we need to book?'

They worked together and soon had a lot of ideas jotted down. The dates weren't yet finalised but it would be about a month away. Plenty of time to get everything organised. With all the new business as well, they offered a job share to two of the *Mums*. They were both highly delighted and arranged their hours between themselves. They both had little ones at the local school and could fetch and carry between themselves as well. It was all very satisfactory.

For the next few weeks, the new Gannets team worked well together. They brought a new cold store and were able to keep many more perishable ingredients in stock. The only social life Zara allowed herself, was the occasional meal out with her father, and Uncle Ted.

'I know you're throwing yourself into it all, but you need a break. Why don't you take a holiday before Lynne's baby arrives?'

'I couldn't possibly. We're much too busy as it is. A new business needs nurturing, as you must know yourself.'

'I'm sure Oliver would love you to join him for a spell in Australia,' Uncle Ted suggested.

'Australia? I don't think so. I haven't got time for even a weekend off at the moment. No chance of a longer holiday. We need to get everything running smoothly before I can think of taking a break. And with Lynne about to disappear, it'll be ages. So, how's your son doing in Australia?'

'Loving it. He seems to think there's a lot of new opportunities out there. But we shall see. I decided I wasn't going back there to live so he's really gone out there to close down my affairs. He'll probably see about putting the house on the market and generally deciding what to do with his life. I suppose you gathered that he was escaping from Amanda? He was pretty angry about the whole business. Then she tried to blackmail him into staying . . . job threats, the lot. Well that was the final straw. He completely lost his temper and walked out there and then.'

'Gosh,' Zara exclaimed, 'I didn't realise that. I just don't understand her motives. She's a nice looking woman and with plenty of money behind her, she surely doesn't have to work so hard to catch a man. Even one as attractive as Oliver.' The two men exchanged glances and her father raised an eyebrow. Sensibly, neither of them made a comment.

'Who knows how women's minds work?'

'You know Tom Asprey pretty well, don't you, Uncle Ted?'

'Certainly. Nice bloke. I was with him at the start of his empire. He was lucky. Got into a field that was going places right at the start.'

'How does he have the time to deal with such minor matters as catering? I mean, for someone who's at the top of the tree, he takes a lot of interest in seemingly unimportant things.'

'He does actually consider welfare to be a major part of his company ethos. He has plenty of experts to deal with all the technical side these days and I suppose you could say he's taken a semi-retirement in a way. He's still very much part of the company but he doesn't travel any more. Amanda swans around most of the time, trying to interfere where she can. Insists on having an office on site. I suppose she

131

thinks it gives her a purpose in life.'

'He's an unusual sort of boss then. I like him a lot.'

It was a good evening and Zara felt refreshed. It was nice to be looked after by two lovely men, even if they were considerably older than her. It was relaxing not to have to be polite all the time or compete with anyone else. It was a small break in an ocean of hard work. Catering was not the easiest occupation to follow.

The residential weekend went better than they could have hoped and even Amanda managed to keep out of the way for most of the time. She was involved in the weekend's business but seemed to have turned her attentions to another new employee who would doubtless be fast-tracked to some elevated position, if she got her way.

'You know at this rate,' Lynne said on the following Monday morning, 'we shall be able to pay off our loans by the end of the year. Who would have thought it?'

'We've been lucky. There was a niche market we were able to fill. If it hadn't been for Asprey's though, we wouldn't be anywhere near where we are today.'

'And it's all thanks to Oliver. And your father.' Zara raised her eyebrows. 'Didn't you realise? They had it all arranged right from the start. But it was us who rose to the challenge. We gave them what they wanted.' They raised their coffee mugs in a toast. 'Here's to us.'

'Back to the slog. I never realised being a company owner made you have perpetually wet hands.'

'Some of us manage to keep dry. Must be delegation.'

'Or pregnancy. Go on, back to the phones, you. We haven't had an order in a while. Well, half an hour at least.' Zara went back to the kitchen and looked at her list. It seemed endless. 'Better busy than not,' she murmured and got on with peeling vegetables for a quiche.

She couldn't take her mind off Oliver for some reason. She kept thinking about ways that she could have handled things differently. Now she would probably never see him again. Maybe Uncle Ted was right and he would like her to go to Australia. Somehow, she doubted it. Besides, it was very hot there and with her fair skin, she'd burn very easily. No, it was a dream she might have had and lost.

She was finally clearing up for the day when her mobile rang. It wasn't a number she recognised.

'Hello?'

'Zara. It's Oliver.'

'Oliver?' she almost shouted down the phone. 'Where on earth are you? This must be costing you a fortune.'

'I'm at home. Well, at Dad's place. I just got back and thought I'd see if you're free for dinner this evening?'

'But you're supposed to be in Australia. Looking at job opportunities.'

'Who told you that? No, I was just having a holiday and sorting out some stuff for Dad. Gave myself time to think. But I got bored with my own company and just thinking so I came back. Landed last night. Or was it this morning? Or is it morning now? I'm totally confused.'

'Sounds as if you need an early night actually, not a dinner date.'

'You could be right. OK. Yes, you are right. I suddenly feel completely drained. But I wanted to speak to you. How are things going?'

'Really well. Asprey's have done us proud. I understand I have you to thank for that. They've been great though. Tom is a love.'

'Yes. Great man. Not like his daughter. Dare I ask how she is?'

'Just busy being Amanda. Whenever I've seen her she's made nasty remarks and she always tries to catch me out. Orders a buffet for fifteen and produces twenty guests plus the odd extra. I'm wise to it now and always take extra portions.'

'Doesn't that affect your profits?'

'Course not. I bill for what they have at a later date. She doesn't deal with the billing any more. And, I think she has her claws into a new man.'

'Poor thing. She should carry a health warning. Look, are you sure about this evening?'

'Quite sure. Maybe I can see you another evening this week?'

'Tomorrow. I'll see you tomorrow. It's so good to talk to you again. Bye.'

'Bye,' Zara whispered and switched off her phone. Her heart was racing. She felt on cloud nine. Oliver was back. He hadn't gone abroad to live after all and he had phoned her almost the first thing after he'd got back. And he wanted to see her.

Perhaps she should have gone out with him this evening but she needed time to absorb the facts. And she must stop talking so nastily about Amanda. After all, Oliver did have some sort of relationship with her. She had the chance to be more generous. On her way home, she stopped off at her father's house.

'Guess what, Dad? Oliver's back.'

'Yes, Darling. I know he is. Did he call you?'

'Just now.'

'Good. He called me to ask if I thought you'd speak to him after all that had happened. I said of course you would. Now, come and sit down and tell me about your day. Glass of wine?'

'Bit early isn't it?'

'Really? No, if you feel you'd like it, then to me it seems like perfect timing. Sit yourself down and I'll see what I've got.'

8

They had a busy morning ahead, but the afternoon was clear the next day. The *Mums* came in to do the bulk of the work so the pressure was off Zara. She went into the office for a coffee and a rest. Excitedly, she told Lynne the news of Oliver's return and said they were going out together that evening.

'I mean, I'm not actually making too much of it but this will be the first time I've seen him since he escaped from Amanda and since I decided he's . . . well . . . he's maybe not so arrogant after all.'

'Oh love, I'm really, really sorry. We've had a late booking. I was coming through to tell you. Someone wants dinner for two. It's not a huge amount of work. We have a lot of it in stock but it will mess up your evening. It's on the other side of town and they want you to serve it. I'm afraid there's no-one else to do it. Unless you want me to go?'

'Course I don't. Mike would kill me if I let you. But curses, I haven't been out for ages. Mind you, Oliver hasn't called again so maybe he's forgotten he asked me out. He was pretty jet-lagged. You'd better give me the list. What do they want?' Lynne handed her the message. 'Oh, at least it's not too bad. I think we've actually got several of these items prepared for later in the week. I'll use them and I can always do more tomorrow.'

She packed up the meal into the various boxes and put them into a large cold box. She prepared a selection of vegetables and packed them too. All she had to do was to heat the main course and cook vegetables when she arrived.

The house was a large old Victorian semi. Rather lovely and with a large sweeping drive. Wonderful. She rang the door bell and went back to the van to collect her cold box.

'Here, let me help you,' said a familiar voice.

'Oliver. What on earth are you doing here?'

'I live here.'

'But I don't understand. I'm supposed to be providing dinner for someone at this address.'

'That's correct.'

'Oh no. You wouldn't do this to me.'

'Do what?'

'Invite me out and then decide you'd rather entertain someone else. It isn't Amanda, is it?'

'Course not. If I never see her again it will be too soon. Come on in. I decided to do the dirty on you and make you cook your own meal. It also means we can talk privately. I asked Lynne to select your favourite things and ask you to bring them over. That way, I could be certain you wouldn't fob me off with another excuse. I've set the table and the kitchen's through there. I hope you don't have a lot to do. I have some champagne ready chilled.

140

Put the food into the oven and come through.'

'Well, this is certainly a first, I've never been invited out to cook my own dinner. And you say Lynne was in on this? Just wait till I get hold of her tomorrow.'

'She was sworn to secrecy. I mean, would you have come at all if you'd known it was me? So I rang and booked you. I know. Awful cheapskate aren't I? Though, actually, the prices you charge aren't that cheap.'

'Naturally. We're very exclusive.'

She organised the meal and went to sit in the comfortable lounge. It was a lovely room with many period features, though it could have done with a lick of paint.

'What do you think of it?' Oliver asked when they were seated on the large sofa.

'Nice. How long have you lived here?'

'Hardly at all. I'd just finalised the deal before the world turned turtle on me. I bought it lock stock and barrel.

I'm deciding what to do with every-thing. The furniture isn't quite me but it sort of fits. Amanda hated it and wanted me to off-load it immediately. Wanted us to live at their place. I was never buying into that though. But enough of all that. It's all in the past. So here we are.'

'You look well. Your break did you good. And you even have a slight tan.'

'And you look quite gorgeous. I'm glad you chose a more casual look for the evening instead of the business suit. Any reason?'

'I wondered if you might phone to invite me out for that meal. I thought I might be clear of this job soon after eight.'

'Instead of which I plan to keep you here for much, much longer than that. Is that all right?'

It felt almost surreal to Zara. She'd thought she was taking a normal booking and now here she was, being her own client. Lynne was quite correct in her choice of menu. They were all things she particularly liked herself. And Oliver was as gorgeous as she remembered. More so. He was funny and entertaining.

'So, am I still as bad as you thought I was?' he asked after the meal.

'What makes you think that?' He mentioned every occasion she had cut him short, complained about him or something he'd done. 'Oh dear. I sound almost as bad as Amanda.'

'Never,' he said. 'Come here.' He put his arms round her and pulled her to him. His kiss sent her floating somewhere above the earth and she wasn't entirely willing to come down. 'Why didn't I realise sooner how very much I love you?' It was approaching midnight before she finally returned home.

'Blow,' she muttered as she climbed into bed. 'I never collected the dishes. Oh well, I'll just have to drive round and collect them tomorrow.' She gave a delighted chuckle as she settled down to remember the wonderful evening.

Lynne was waiting anxiously the next morning.

'How did it go? No, don't answer that. One look at your face tells me.'

'You're a wicked, devious woman, do you know that?' Zara chided.

'I know. Great isn't it? And being so pregnant you can't tell me off as I mustn't be upset.'

'Honestly. You are the limit.'

'But you'd never have gone if I'd spoilt the surprise. And I bet it was a wonderful meal. I knew it was going to be a good thing when he asked for dishes that went with champagne.'

'Naturally. Oh Lynne, he's just gorgeous. Why on earth didn't I see it before? Oh yes, I'm sorry but I left the dishes and everything there. I'll have to go and collect them later.'

'No you won't. I've delivered them back personally.' He was standing in the doorway clad in his off duty denims and wearing what Amanda had declared was

144

designer stubble.

'Oliver. Good morning.'

'Don't mind me,' Lynne said, as he leaned over to kiss Zara.

'Thought I'd drop them off personally. I put them through my dishwasher so they're nice and clean. And I've come to settle my bill.'

'Don't be silly,' Zara told him. 'We couldn't charge you.'

'And here I thought you were thoroughly professional and I might be marrying into a successful business. Then you could keep me in the way to which I was once accustomed.'

'Marrying?' Lynne squeaked. 'You never mentioned that. You never said you were getting married.'

'I er . . . are we? Did I miss something last night?'

'Maybe I forgot to ask you. Excuse us, Lynne. Zara, please say you'll marry me.'

'Of course she will,' Lynne burst out. Zara glared. 'Don't be stupid, Zara. Course she'll marry you. She's nuts about you.'

'Do I get any say in this?' Zara tried to sound angry.

'No. I'm the senior partner and what I say goes. Besides, I'm pregnant and mustn't be upset. Remember?'

'You're not the senior partner. We're equals.'

'Yes, but I am six months older than you. That makes me your senior.'

'Ladies, ladies, please. Maybe we should let Zara answer. Well?'

'I suppose so.'

'You are just too enthusiastic,' grumbled Lynne. 'If a gorgeous hunk asked me to marry him, I'd be drooling by now.'

'Thought you were happily married? Yes, Oliver, of course I'll marry you. Though I could think of a more romantic time and place to be asked. And without my nosy friend as chief witness to it all.'

'Thank goodness for that. Now, we need to organise the engagement party. Date? Menu? And where should we hold it?' Lynne had already pulled out her pad and pen.

'Actually, I'd rather not have a party,' Oliver announced. 'If that's OK with you two. The last party was just too traumatic.'

'But that one was never meant to be an engagement party.'

'I know. But actually, I have to find a job first. I'd like to stay in this area but I'm not sure what I shall be doing. I know you are committed here but I bought the house on the strength of the job at Asprey's and now I doubt I can afford it. Unless you're a wealthy lady and have been hiding it?'

'Would I be slogging away producing dinner parties for lonely bachelors if I was rich?' Zara retorted. 'But, me and the bank do own part of my flat. You could move in there.'

'Don't be ridiculous,' Lynne told her. 'You've hardly got any space for one let alone two. And the business is doing OK but it won't pay off the loans for another few months. You could always work as a waiter for us.'

'Hold the job. Mind you, it might be

the best offer I get. But, the upshot is that I don't want a party, if that's OK with you, Zara?'

'Absolutely fine. We could have a celebratory dinner party for the Fathers and Lynne and Mike of course.'

'Sounds wonderful. Don't tell them why though. Let's announce it together.'

They went into planning mode and within minutes, had the menu and date decided and agreed to hold the dinner party at Oliver's house.

'We might as well, while I still have it. So, I'll see you the day after tomorrow. If you can spare her Lynne, can I take Zara out to do some shopping tomorrow afternoon?' Beaming with joy, Lynne agreed.

'Can I just remind you that you do have a booking tomorrow? At Asprey's. You should be clear by two-thirty.'

'Maybe I could come and be the waiter,' Oliver suggested. 'You did offer me a job.'

'I think that might be rubbing salt into the wound. Now, you'd better go away or I shall never finish everything I have to do.'

'Is this the way it's going to be? Engaged for all of five minutes and I'm being dismissed.'

'If you will propose, if that's what it can be called, right after breakfast on a working day, what can you expect? You can stay and peel potatoes if you like.'

'I'd better go and buy some newspapers and see what jobs are going if I'm to have a wife to support . . . all right. I'm going. I love you.'

'Well thank you,' said Lynne. 'I'm quite keen on you too but I am married and very pregnant.'

'Cheek,' laughed Zara. 'And you don't need to keep mentioning your pregnancy. It sticks out a mile. Literally.'

* * *

The day passed in a haze of delight, disbelief and hard work. It was a finger buffet the following day and required a large array of small items which always took lots of time. But, once made, it was easy to set out and serve and quick to clear up. The profiteroles were served in their individual dishes so again, convenient to serve.

'You should be clear easily by two. The *Mums* can sort out the dirty things when you get back and you can go off on your romantic mission. I'm so happy for you.'

'I'm happy for me too. I never realised how much I could love someone.'

'Go home and take the stars in your eyes with you. Frankly, I'm beginning to feel quite jealous.'

* * *

Oliver was spending the evening with his father to catch up on the details of his trip to Australia. Uncle Ted had finally decided he would stay in England and Oliver was supposed to be winding up all his affairs out there. She hoped he could keep their big news secret until the dinner party.

As Zara drove to Asprey's the next day, she remembered that first drive there. Just about here that Oliver scraped her van and she took an immediate dislike to him for his lack of courtesy. As she went inside, she remembered the first time she had seen him with all his colleagues and thought what a handsome man he was. Then she realised it was he who had scraped her car and failed to stop and had decided he was an arrogant, spoiled brat.

'Morning, Zara,' Geoff called. She came down to earth.

'Hi, Geoff. How are you?'

'Fine. I hear Mr Pendlebury's back.'

'How on earth do you know that?'

'Excellent grapevine we have here. Someone saw him in the town yesterday. I fancy her ladyship will be waiting with her claws out.'

'Thought she had a new man in tow?'

'Couldn't stay the course. Now,

you're to use the boardroom annex today. Jenny's set up the coffee already and bottles of water. All you need to do is unload your stuff from the van and I'll take you and your trolley up in the service lift.'

'I thought it was the usual buffet?'

'Directors.'

'Oh dear. I hope it's grand enough for them. We weren't told it was a special occasion.'

'Don't suppose it is, Mr Tom's always one for informality. That's why they didn't want a sit down meal. More chat carried out over casual food than anywhere else apparently.'

Tom Asprey came over to chat to her as soon as he saw her.

'Zara. How are you? I hear Oliver's back in town?'

'Yes. He came back a couple of days ago.'

'Is he going to stay in these parts?'

'I think so. If he can get a job.'

'So, not staying in Australia after all? I thought he left to take up something over there. Some super job he couldn't turn down. That's what the word is.'

'Actually, if you don't mind my saying it,' she paused and glanced round to make sure Amanda wasn't in earshot, 'it was because Amanda told him to go. If he wasn't prepared to marry her, then she suggested there was no place for him at Asprey's.'

He drew in his breath and the colour rose in his cheeks. 'I see. I suspected as much. My daughter has a lot to answer for. She's taking a long holiday in the Mediterranean with friends. I felt she needed to get right away for a while.' He looked furious, despite his mild words. 'I take it you're in contact with Oliver?'

'Actually, we . . . yes, I have seen him.'

'Tell him to arrange an appointment. I'd like to have him back on board. Does he still have the same phone number?'

'I'm not sure.' She remembered he had called her the other day and pulled out her mobile. The number was logged. She found it and gave it to Tom.

'Good. I'll call him as soon as we're done here. Thanks, Zara. Nice food, as usual. Just right for us. Now, you must excuse me.'

She finished her work and could hardly wait to see Oliver and tell him the good news. Everything was working out. She had almost let the cat out of the bag to Tom, about their engagement. Their fathers must be the first to know. They would both be delighted, she was certain.

Oliver was waiting at the kitchen when she arrived back there.

'Come on. Let's get the van unloaded and then we can be off. It might take some time to choose a ring. I know what you women are like. Do you have anything in mind?'

'Of course not. I've been too busy.'

'You do want to choose it yourself, don't you? I mean, I could have got something but I wasn't sure what you'd like.'

'This is perfect,' she assured him. 'I'd have been happy either ways. Now, am I allowed to get a word in? I've just been to Asprey's, and had an interesting talk with Tom. He wants you to give him a call. Actually, he might call you later. I think you're going to be offered your job back. He was pretty angry when he discovered it was Amanda's doing that made you leave. She'd suggested you'd been offered something spectacular in Australia, I gather.'

'Amanda's imagination once more.' His mobile rang. 'Excuse me,' he said.

Zara carried on unloading the van and took it into the washing up area. One of the *Mums* was working and began to put the dishes into the machine.

'All go well, did it?'

'Splendidly,' Zara said with a grin. She went outside again. Oliver was still on the phone, but he caught her hand to delay her.

'Thanks, Tom. That's really great. I'll see you very soon.' He switched off the call and turned to Zara, a broad grin on his face. 'Tom's offered me my old job back and wants me to go in right away to sign a new contract. I know we were supposed to be going shopping but I can't really say no. Is it all right?'

'Of course,' she said, trying to hide her disappointment. 'You must go. It's most important.'

'Thank you, Darling. You're amazing.' He kissed her cheek and dashed off to his car. He hooted as he drove away. Feeling let down, she went back inside and slumped down in the office.

'What's up?' Lynne asked. 'Where's the man? And the ring?'

'Job opportunity came up. Ring's on hold.'

'But that's great. Think about it. You'll have a home to live in after all. You'll still get your ring.'

'Not before the dinner party though. We'll be too busy to go shopping tomorrow. I so wanted to wear it tomorrow and let the fathers see it before we said anything.'

'You can borrow mine if that's the only problem.'

'Oh, Lynne, you are a dear. But it isn't important. They'll be thrilled with the news, ring or no ring. Now, I have a free afternoon after all. What shall I do towards tomorrow?'

9

As the meal was ending, Oliver stood up and chinked a spoon against his glass. 'We have an announcement,' he began.

'I thought you'd never get round to it,' moaned Lynne. 'I've been biting my tongue all evening, trying not to drop any hints.'

'Hush, Lynne. This isn't your party,' Mike told her. She glowered and was about to let them know she shouldn't be upset due to her pregnancy but he kissed her to keep her quiet.

'Zara has agreed to be my wife and I am going back to Asprey's to my old job.'

Both fathers rose and went to the other's child.

'Oliver, I'm delighted, my boy,' said Zara's father.

'Zara, my dear, it's what I'd always

hoped for. Oliver's mother and yours always felt the same way. They'll probably be looking down on us saying well done.' He looked down at her ring finger. 'Not been shopping yet?'

'It got cancelled,' she said with a grin.

'Then perhaps you'd like this one.' He fished inside his shirt and drew out a chain with a ring threaded on it.

'Mum's ring,' Oliver exclaimed. 'I wondered what happened to it.'

'I've worn it ever since she died. I think it was ready for you, Zara, my dear. I was keeping it warm for you. It will do till this son of mine takes you out to buy a new one.' He handed it to Oliver and he slipped it on her finger. It was a perfect fit.

'Thank you so much. If it's all right with Oliver, I'd be proud for this to be my ring. If you're certain you don't mind being parted from it. I won't be needing another one.'

'I knew I'd found a thrifty woman,' Oliver said proudly.

'Ouch,' moaned Lynne. 'I shouldn't

have eaten a second helping.'

'What is it? Are you all right?' Mike asked anxiously.

'No. I'm not. I've got the most violent stomach pains. That pheasant must have been off. I'm sorry but I might be sick any moment. What's the matter? Why are you all laughing at me? I'm dying here.'

'And you're pregnant, Lynne. Remember?'

'Of course I am. I can hardly forget it. Ouch,' she moaned again.

'And what happens at the end of a pregnancy?'

'You mean? Oh my goodness. You mean I'm . . . but it isn't time yet. There's another week to go.'

'Let's get you to hospital. You're in labour.'

'But I haven't got my bag. Haven't got anything. Mike. Do something.'

'Now where's that calm, serene friend I used to have?' teased Zara. 'Go on Mike. Cart her away. We'll go and collect your bags and bring them to the hospital. I should have known you'd try to upstage my big announcement.'

'Ouch, ouch,' Lynne moaned as Mike led her to the door.

'We'll be back in a little while. Help yourself to another drink,' Oliver told the two fathers.

It was an hour by the time they had collected Lynne's bag, driven it to the hospital and got back to Oliver's house. Their fathers were sitting by the fire drinking brandy.

'You look cosy,' Zara said fondly.

'We've been having a chat and a think. Ted's been renting his place since his return from Australia. While he made up his mind what to do, I'm rattling around in my place since I've been living on my own.'

'Hope it's all right with you, Zara, but we've decided he could move in with me. Your old room will always be there for you but there's another double room and plenty of space for us both to have a study each. What do you think?'

'I think it's the best idea you could

have had. It'll be great for you to have each other's company and somewhere to be on your own when you want it.'

'And you're sure you don't mind?'

'Of course not. Why would I?'

'Well, it might seem I was trying to usurp your old home. After all, it will be yours one day,' Uncle Ted suggested.

'Not for very many years I hope. Besides, this will be my home soon. Assuming this son of yours agrees to change this wallpaper. It's horrible.'

They chatted happily of the future and the many possibilities for them all. Zara spent most of the time glancing at her watch and picking up her mobile to see if there had been a call that she could possibly have missed.

'I can see your mind is occupied elsewhere,' Oliver said at around eleven o'clock. 'Why don't we drive to the hospital? We can wait with Mike until there's some news.'

'Do you mind? After all, this is my godchild we're waiting for. Is that OK, you two?'

'Time I was getting home,' said her father. 'You don't mind dropping me off, do you, Ted?'

They abandoned the dirty dishes and left everything on the table and Oliver drove his new fiancée to the hospital. They dashed to the reception desk in the maternity unit and announced their arrival.

'We don't usually allow visitors at this time of night,' the nurse said.

'But this is my godchild. Please, can't you at least tell us how Lynne is?'

'She's fine,' Mike said as he joined them. 'And so is the most beautiful little girl I've ever seen. She looks just like her mother.'

'Congratulations,' they said in unison as they hugged the new father.

'What a day,' Zara nodded. 'Truly the beginning of a whole new era. I'd suggest champagne but I know Lynne would never forgive me if she missed out on it.'

Other titles in the
Linford Romance Library:

FALLING LEAVES

Sheila Benton

When Richard employs Annie to update the computer system for his company, she finds herself, through circumstance, living in his house. Although they are attracted to each other, Richard's daughter, Katie, takes a dislike to her. Added to this, Annie suspects that Richard is in love with someone else, so she allows herself to be drawn to Steve, Richard's accountant. Annie feels she must choose between love and a career — how can the complications in her life be resolved . . . ?

THE BUTTERFLY DANCE

Rosemary A. Smith

It's 1902 and life, for Katherine Johnson, has been rather mundane, living with her Aunt Phoebe and Uncle Zachariah in their house on the coast. However, on her twentieth birthday, she meets Kane O'Brien on the beach and suddenly her thoughts are all of him. But will the circumstances of Kane's birth prevent her Aunt from accepting their love for one another? What is the mystery of the beautiful keepsake box? And where will the butterfly dance lead them?